RODGER WASHINGTON

Missouri Man

This novel is entirely a work of fiction. The names, characters and incidents portrayed in it are the work of the author's imagination. Any resemblance to actual persons, living or dead, events or localities is entirely coincidental.

Rodger Washington asserts the moral right to be identified as the author of this work.

First edition

ISBN: 9798452123279

Cover art by Rodger Washington

This book was professionally typeset on Reedsy.
Find out more at reedsy.com

Contents

I

The Missouri Man Part One

1

The Bottom

She never stood a chance. There were always too many people that could do what she could. Nothing stood out about her. Tangible attributes of greatness weren't apparent. She was most people. The bottom is crowded. All are at the bottom. There is too much to deal with at the bottom. Those at the bottom are constricted by the tentacles of pay day loans with predatory rates. The meat lacks quality coupled with a lack of fresh vegetables. At the bottom the bank doubles as the liquor store. The American dream is pursued in the form of past lottery winning number patterns scribbled in an old notebook. Surely there has to be a pattern yet to be unlocked. True wealth couldn't be random. The bottom knows no true privacy. Her morning transit to meager earnings was shared with the public. Different energies flowed around her at the bottom unable to be ignored. Every morning there were forced unavoidable conversations. Public transportation isn't equipped with an atmosphere of morning reflection. The bottom doesn't allot for introspection and reflection, only motion. Wake up. Eat. Shower. Run for the bus. Stand if there is no seat. Ignore the creep who won't accept "no". Watch over yourself. Protect yourself. Stay alert. Make sure you aren't followed. You've arrived at work. Work. Eat what you can afford. Work. Your feet don't hurt. Ignore your pains. Don't dream, it's dangerous. Walk home. Watch over yourself. Have your keys out. Protect yourself. Stay alert. He was standing there last night. Remember his face. Don't make eye contact, he'll speak. Where are your keys? Tighten the grip on your purse. You're almost home. The street light is out. Ignore the pain. Your feet don't hurt you are 3 minutes away from your door. Why is he walking in the same direction as you? Your feet CAN'T hurt now. Don't make noise the stray dog could bite. You're home. That's one with only a lifetime to go.

    The bottom is a balancing act like no other. For every action there was a complete over reaction at the bottom. A boy would have candy other boys couldn't purchase. The boy with the candy had better finish it close to the store or hide it on the walk back up the block. The choice was his on how to proceed with his gifted glucose. Balance out the repercussions of walking back up the street with something the others wanted. Is today the day to possibly fight for this? Would winning the fight be worth the trouble? Do you have enough to share with the other boys? Will they allow you to share? If you do share would it make you look soft to them? The boy could just put the candy in his pocket but what if the boys saw him go to the store? Surely you didn't walk in just to sight see; a purchase must have been made. The desire would be to eat the candy while watching the game but was the neighborhood offering this option? The bottom is a balancing act indeed. She saw these and other scenarios her entire life from the window. Her reality dulled her personality. Her brown eyes were void of joy since as a child she was told the amusement park didn't have a ticket for her. Her mother told her at 9 that the amusement park had sold all of its tickets before it opened that season. She wasn't lucky enough to have the extra income to get the tickets when they first hit the market. All the families in the amusement park were able to buy tickets for the upcoming summer. A family vehicle ensured other families were able to be at the ticket booth long before tickets were to be sold. The same car allotted those families ability to work further from home enabling them to generate more funds. The tickets other families purchased represented to her a lack of ability. How lucky they were to be able. She knew how to have a form of fun with the world she had. Drawing the people outside the window was fun. They were all characters after all. The neighborhood was packed with amusement. There was no better entertainment than the people. Young empty bellied teenagers stealing hubcaps and selling them to auto shops, only for the auto shop to sell them back to other people who were able to buy discounted rims after theirs had been stolen during the time of no error. Economic lessons of the boom and bust cycle could be absorbed tuition free from the kitchen window.

No more pertinent applicable knowledge was attainable from the window then that of human psychology. People who were able to make their way to the neighborhood to purchase a few moments of euphoria unconsciously applied as case studies. She was often in awe of the many tourists that came back unaware of the low quality of the momentary magic they risked their all for. It would be years before she would realize those people found part of their zeal in the transaction itself. Thrill seeking through proximity to systemic despair and dangers provided releases of hormones as would escaping a lion's jaw moments before it closed down on one's leg. These lessons and more when learned in real time were the ultimate fun. "Fun is after all what you make it" she concluded as others regaled her with amusement park exaggerations. Her quick witted defense often reminded her of how much fun the amusement park would be on days it rained. The kitchen window never closed due to weather. The show would stall but never end. She defiantly concluded as a child her truth that; the amusement park could never beat the kitchen window.

As a 20 year old, the bottom offered at the very least consistency. She knew going to the liquor store for snacks near 5 p.m. on a Wednesday would cause her to stand longer. Lottery players would occupy the front glass for what seemed like an eternity. There they stood with their journals filled with previous winning numbers and dates unconcerned of who might have only two items to purchase. She hated their false sense of optimism. What level of angst one must feel; exhausting multiple series of numbers seeking to find the pattern that would reveal the next fortune producer. She saw how tight the old man held onto this notebook. She held a frown as a teen at how it was held so close to his rib. This poor old man. To him the secret to life had been inked on its pages. He only had to figure out its code. She felt for him and those like him. Moreover, she found herself irritated by the time it took to choose the numbers his kind gave their funds to.

"How is it you have a formula but you're still up there taking forever to pick what numbers you want? If it's a formula you know what you need before you come in the damn store!" No response from the old man was directed to the irritated girl. He was focused on his investing process and lacked concern for the common customers. "That is so annoying it takes those lotto players forever!" The store clerk Monty laughed and retorted to her, "he has a formula but when he gets up here with that poor lil social security check, he always changes his mind on the numbers. I swear he has paid the lotto people enough to buy a speedboat by now. He's been doing that for at least 25 years. Poor guy believes his numbers will hit though and hey, gotta believe in something." The girl sarcastically smirked at Monty on the other side of the glass. "You don't really believe his actions make sense do you? You know he's wasting his money right? And what's the odds on someone hitting the lottery? Like seriously and then someone from here? Come on now man. You know better." Monty shrugged as he slid her change through the open slot under the glass. She was too intelligent to waste her funds on pipe dreams. She knew how hard it was to make and keep a dollar. Silly dreams were expensive. If one could be consistent at least trouble could be minimized. Survival is all about consistency. Her mother told her always to save whatever was possible. Save even if it was 5$. Save it anyway. Growing up the girl didn't honestly comprehend why her mother was so adamant on saving but she respected the source and never strayed from the lesson. She saved every extra dime she could for years. There was no target date. There was no dollar goal. She didn't count the savings often but had a rough running estimate after every fold able or jingling deposit. For five years she had been employed and had saved a total of $2953.82 give or take. She knew her shoe box wealth far surpassed many around her. She knew how to be consistent. She knew her mother told her that to save was vital. She simply didn't know what precisely she would do with the money nor did she know when she would do it. She was for now merely content with the fact that she had it. "They canceled the overtime girl. This big ass company and they're cutting back. It's a trip." Vanessa's friend and coworker

Mya ruined her day with the news. "I was supposed to get like 10 hours of OT this week, look at these nails girl. I am not a boxer why do my hands look like this? They messing with the church's money now Ness." Vanessa broke her gaze of the parking lot to give attention to her friend's minor crisis. "Now Mya. We both know if you only worked 10 hours a year you would be getting those claws done, stop fronting like that overtime is keeping you out of that nail shop. What time is your appointment girl?" Mya laughingly replied, "ha whatever heifer. 1 pm dang. Stop acting like you know me!" The two young women laughed as they gathered themselves to return from their short nearly fifteen minute break. Vanessa had planned as well for overtime to continue through the week. She wasn't as concerned about getting her nails done. She hoped for enough to purchase art supplies she would be longing for nearly all year. "I'm tired of being here. Tired of this job. I don't know what I want yet but I know I don't want this." Vanessa's patience with her current circumstance wore more thin by the day. Mya nervously nudged her friend in her side. Fighting her caution she asked, "Ness you want to come to this party with me?" The offer seemed reasonable enough.

2

The Father

"OK brothers now for those who can, write on this paper. What would you do for your son?" The father looked at the blank paper and around the room at all the other fathers. Some of them were able to write, some were not. The literacy rate in State prison is astoundingly low. Jeff could write. He could read as well. He didn't lack those basic yet necessary skills. He simply wasn't comfortable with the subject matter. "Jeff? You cool man?" Hank was a good guy. In private Jeff could call him Hank. But with other inmates around it was always officer Denton. There isn't much privacy in prison. Hearing his name, Jeff departed from his entranced state. "Yeah officer D, I'm cool. I think I'm just gonna sit this one out." Officer Denton understood. Jeff watched the group of men writing about what they would do for their sons. Some of the men looked focused, some looked confused. All looked pathetic. None of them could do anything for their sons because they were all property of the state. These men dreamed of being on the sideline as their son scored a point, or showing them how to change a tire on the family car. They imagined watching their son win or lose their first scuffle with some boy down the street who would later become the boys' friend for life. Dreams haunt men that have no ability to chase them. Jeff tried often not to dream. He boxed and ran instead.

A fellow inmate asked, "Jeff what did you put? What did you say you would do for E.J.?" The father seemed to whisper to the world his response, "Everything man." Jeff Jacobs was the best father he could be considering the circumstances. He made every call he was allowed and could afford to his son. There were weeks he would call Eric up to eight times. He gave all the advice his time allowed during brief phone calls. After his phone call ended, Jeff had to allow another man to raise his son via stern and hopeful conversation. The father looked at the clock the second guard was standing under. Officer Denton internalized Jeff's angst and reported to the class, "alright guys that's it today. More on Wednesday, try to think of something!" The room slowly cleared. "Wait hold up we still got 10 minutes left before yard time. What's that about man." Devon always pushed every issue he could. It was his nature. Jeff slowed up in order to put the chairs back. "Aye naw man put the chairs back we still got 10 minutes before yard time officer. We don't have to leave yet do we? Damn man your shift almost over dude. What's the rush?" Devon had a way of making calm men uneasy. Jeff, sensing the tensions attempted to calm the situation. "Hey officers next group maybe let us go 10 minutes over?" To the group Officer Denton replied, Wednesday we will clear it for us to go 10 over ONLY IF none of you have any incidents in the next 2 days gentlemen. It's on you."

The majority of the men nodded their heads in agreement. Devon though was unsatisfied with the calm. "I'm saying, we're already here now though. Wednesday might not even come. We should seize the day n all that right? Let's just gone head and finish it today. I need to, you know open up and get better too" he sarcastically sputtered. Devon was as good as he would ever be. There was no reason to be better than he was. The prison was his and he had a life to be the feeble minded king over it. Other prisoners of a weaker mindset often not only followed his lead but took the fall for him to stay in his good graces. Devon, better known to many on the outside as Red Dot always seemed to escape any situation unscathed. Jeff grew weary of this unnecessary disagreement. Moreover this was one of the few times he could speak privately with Hank; his friend of sorts.

"D, its only a few minutes man. Come Wednesday we'll be glad we pushed the time out." Red dot turned quickly from the others and glared at Jeff. "Pushed the time out? You think that's funny G? That's a joke to you?" Devon had been in prison for 6 years when he was found guilty of three previous crimes totaling a life sentence as well as another 20 years. He had appeals left but hope was gone from him. Upon receiving the news Devon beat a fellow inmate within an inch of his life. When asked why, he said the man stole his cigarettes though Devon had never smoked a day in his life. Already unable to read well and having no skills he quickly thrived in what would be his new home. He fully transitioned to what he had only dabbled in previously. He was a man of no light. Jeff felt his anger rise from the depth of his soul. Though he knew Red Dot's status, Jeff was not one to be tested by another. His anger was calm but sincere, and difficult to resign. Jeff looked at Red Dot and his flunkies with a fury that made others uneasy. "D, don't take me the wrong way. Let's just finish it Wednesday man. It's all good. Be cool though man. For real be cool." Jeff didn't care to be spoken to in a certain tone by another man. He went out of his way to show respect so that if ever there was an issue he knew it wasn't because he had over reacted. Jeff had only reacted, never acted initially. This is what he was raised to do and this surely absolved him. How could one not be vindicated? Any actions taken on his part were spurred from confrontation he never began. If there was ever violence it was always because Jeff had to respond. The motto he lived by was simply, *the stronger man ends it.* Red Dot was respected by the fellow inmates, but Jeff received a different type of respect that Red Dot could not understand, or be at peace with. Jeff had no interest in position, status or power. Red Dot dreamed of nothing less. Jeff's internal peace disturbed him. It confused him. Confusion is the base ingredient for the compound of fear. Jeff was therefore a problem. Red Dot concluded that the only men that don't crave power already have it.

Jeff walked toward Devon who was surprised at Jeff's complete reckless abandon. Red Dot moved toward Jeff before Officer Denton bellowed "The hole is waiting to see how stupid you fellas wanna be today! Cool off now!" Two more guards moved toward Red Dot, causing his 3 sheepish followers to respond to their aggressive stance. "Naw its cool all good bruh." Devon said in a low tone toward the officers. His men immediately stood down as to deescalate the situation. Jeff had not moved. He stood with the weight of the world tightly clinched in his left fist ever prepared to unleash it. Still ready to end it. Officer Denton noticed the father unmoved by the new pseudo calm. "Hey Jeff you too. Cool it. Pack up fellas. Everyone cool off." The officers ensured Devon and his crew exited the room as Jeff and a handful of others straightened the area up after the group. As the majority of inmates left Hank said to the father what he knew he would.

"You can't let your mind depress you because you're not able to be there for him. You have to stay strong mentally just as you do physically for when you're back out in the world. Damn it Jeff you can't let the world know where you stand all the time." The father knew Hank was right. He also knew Hank would be at hockey practice with his son by 7:00 p.m. He managed to reply, "Hank I'm trying man, but I'll give it more." Hank, realizing Jeff's vulnerability, patted his back and silently understood. Officer Denton understood that the father was a fighter. He had the soul of a fighter. Any fighter's strength will waiver when hit in the right places though. The father had one place left, his son Eric.

3

Grad School

"Phil, you ready man? Come on stop looking for the easy out, its time to work out bro!" Eric, like his father, was a natural fighter. He found peace in pain. Pain is familiar and who likes surprises? Eric was a beautiful fighter, but as Gordy always told him, he was missing something. His natural gifts though could make up for his missing element in the ring. Phil, Eric's best friend was not a fighter. He enjoyed the fatter things. He was athletic, but only until he got tired, and for most of his life he was OK with that. "E.J. man look I'm tired already dude, don't be having me running hills and knocking down buildings then screaming that's just a warm up OK! I'm warm already, don't start bruh. I don't wanna hear it. Don't try to kill me today with this eye of the lion and all that raging bear crap. I'm already tired man. Matter of fact never mind let's go get some wings and get on this game." Eric laughed at his best friend's willingness to be defeated. "You know what they'll say about you Phillip Rogers? They will say we never knew how good he could be in life because he took the easy route. That needs to bother you more than it does bruh. Let's get it." Phil reluctantly closed his gym locker and followed his friend into the lair.

To consider the lair a massive gym was an understatement. It was large in square foot, but it was huge in legend. The lair started as an abandoned factory. It hadn't been used for manufacturing for so many years that most remembered it as merely abandoned. That was until Chipper Harris Mason arrived. Chipper Harris Mason made tens of millions of dollars helping develop an app that grew so popular that he and his 3 friends sold it to what they considered an idol in Silicon Valley. Chipper was one of the few people that looked like him to ever come from where he came from and do what he did in business and technology. His greatest feat in his personal opinion was not amassing great wealth nor was it his philanthropy. His highest level of achievement was his source of inspiration in creating the lair. It was that he came back home no longer obese. Chips, as they called him, went off to college a whopping 287 pounds. He loved every food he could pronounce, and his pronunciation was keen. Chips would be a bright big guy most of his early life, until he met his 3 friends. All of them came from a different athletic background. Lisa Ramirez had kick boxed since she could crawl. Much like Eric Jacobs, her father was a fighter for a short time in history as well. She was once told by a staffer that she was now an example to young women that operated in boardrooms full of middle-aged men. Before she could determine how to process this, the aid continued with what would instantly disgruntle her. It was a suggestion that kick boxing should be replaced with yoga. She didn't want to be perceived as difficult or hostile for fear others wouldn't want to partner. Moreover, God forbid she walk into a room with a scratch, bruise or blemish on her face. Peers could be uncomfortable. It would be unbecoming. Lisa's reply to the aid was simply, "I already became."

Simon Sandroni was a cross fit enthusiast. He also mountain biked every chance he could in the most dangerous environ- ments he could be dropped in. He surfed when there were warnings to stay on the shore. He climbed mountains with minimal resources and no guide. The mundane insulted him. He lived to disrupt, rather it be companies or any other societal norm. His spirit was wild and unable to be tamed. Fringe thrill and victory appealed to Simon and nothing more. Pushing the envelope had grown to be cliché in a world full of pretenders. Simon tore the envelope apart daily. He was talented but he was dark. Asked once why he had a death wish he replied, "I don't have a death wish. I have a death guarantee. We all do. A fool lives a life attempting to avoid the inevitable."

The largest fan of all things sport was Ralph Mitchell. All through his youth Ralph would compare his frame to his peers. He hated the small calves and narrow shoulders he had been designed with. Powerful men look powerful. At the age of 14 he decided to take matters into his own hands through strict dieting and a devoted weight lifting regimen. In two short years he would gain nearly 28 pounds of muscle and a world of confidence. He loved to keep cut with swimming. The pool is where he assisted Chips in shedding his excess. When Chips began to spend his time with these three future industry disruptors, more than his brain would be worked out. Within 2 years he had lost 87 pounds. He thrived among like minds.

A few years later these four friends would sell an app and the intellectual property attached for 750 million dollars to an engineering legend in Silicon Valley that any of them would have been overwhelmed to even intern for. Now two years removed from undergrad, Chips was a fit newly minted multimillionaire wanting to provide access for everyone from his city to work out and brainstorm. Often while driving about his city his mind repeated the same questions. Why not us? Why not here? Before he bought his own home, he rushed to purchase abandoned buildings and the surrounding property near it. After speaking with developers and city planning committees, he successfully turned his new purchase into a 4 level gym in the middle of a sprawling campus. The state of the art campus was nothing short of phenomenal. The Lair's first floor had 2 pools 2 saunas and an area for yoga. The second floor fit 3 full size basketball courts as well as an area for chess to be played. The third floor was a standard gym that left nothing to be desired. It had ropes to climb to the ceiling. It held every form of fitness machinery imaginable. The weights were always in pristine order when unused and there were 8 massage chairs in a separate room. Eric and Phil had come to the fourth floor.

The fourth floor had been named by Chips himself. *College.* This was the boxing and Mixed Martial Arts gym. College had all the state of the art boxing equipment. Dozens of pairs of leather gloves lined a wall ready to be used to teach young sparring partners more about themselves than they ever knew. Several heavy and speed Bags hung from the ceiling having never lost a fight. There were 3 smaller rings known affectionately as classrooms. Where every fighter wanted to be on a Friday night though, was the center of the college. In the center of the college the large ring awaited those who the Dean deemed prepared for the most prolific of destructive dissertations. The main ring had been affectionately named *Grad School.*

The fights that took place in Grad school were those of legend. Many successful professional fighters came to grad school and educated or at times were even themselves refreshed. Grad school is where the son aspired to be. He had 3 impediments

17

preventing him from enrolling in the middle of the main ring. His first problem was his anger. When the son felt pain, he felt it his duty to immediately respond. This caused him to rush his next punch. One can imagine how that would usually end for the young *college* student. His second problem, in his own mind, was Gordy. Gordy was 47 years old but he looked younger. His few grey hairs were more so platinum. He was the Dean of the University of boxing. The College was his world and he ruled it with cunning, witty jokes and a spry pugilistic mind. Gordy was a thinking man. He wanted Eric to be a thinking man while in motion. He would scold the son for relying on athleticism over his mind during a fight. The son and the Dean clashed without cease. This caused Eric to repeat entire courses of pain in the ring. The two were vinegar and oil. The third reason for not being admitted into grad school was Pierre. Pierre the Prowler Sultan. This was the man's real name. He ruled grad school as a sultan would, with all poise and power. The pirate had never lost. Not only had he never lost, he never really came close to losing a fight. It made him hated, loathed and reverenced. The Dean admired Sultan's work but would never train him solely. He said that it just wasn't to be. The sultan taking offense promised to knock out any fighter Gordy showed his affection to. It was during a training session that Pierre noticed Gordy's watchful eye on Eric. Jealousy overtook Sultan instantly. Unknowingly the son had made an enemy.

Eric had not had the chance to ask before he heard, "Not yet and stop questioning me son. When you are truly ready I will know it, not you." Gordy hastily attempted to set the son back on track for the day's work. His comedic wit attempted another method. "Phil you still fat? Sheesh boy! I mean you are still fat! Still fat Phil, I can always count on you Phil to be still fat.

18

I look at my stock options every day, they change. Weather? Changes. My woman's hair, changes... too much. Not you Phil, I depend on you still fat Phil, to never change. You can though, we won't charge you any extra if you do change you know. It's OK to be fit Phillip." Gordy patted his stomach as he looked at Phil's stomach and laughed. "I'm a few rounds away from fighting 50 years old. You are a young man and I just wonder when are you gonna take off that extra fur coat youngster? Get to work. Jump rope is calling your name. Keep your chin up. I don't want your flabby chest hitting you in the chin knocking you out before you ever get the gloves on!" Phil reluctantly stepped away from the row of gloves and toward the mirror where he was to jump rope. Phil enjoyed jumping rope. Quietly he enjoyed the swimming laps, the weights the road work. He enjoyed all things training. He simply enjoyed it for a short time. After a short time he decided he was tired but proud. Eric was always proud of Phil for simply showing up. That was enough for Eric. Just show up. You have no choice but win if you just show up consistently. Wouldn't showing up without fail eventually equate to victories? Isn't Phil doing himself a great disservice by not at least putting up the effort he does? He could be worse off if not for this minimal commitment. Shouldn't that be praised? If Phil's minimal commitment is praised it will surely pay dividends that will compound into more commitment. This must be true. Isn't it? Eric had faith in the dependability of Phil's halfhearted effort. It never succeeded but it never failed. The glass was half full. Eric dare not ask more of him.

Gordy was no friend of Phil. Nor did Gordy make excuses for him. Gordy had seen this all his life; a man not living to his full potential yet hoping for maximum results. He was hard on Phil as he was his serious students who showed potential to compete. Those students though loved to have Gordy breathing down their necks. They outworked each other for his approval. It was inconceivable for them to comprehend why Gordy would ever waste an insult on the half hearted. How had he earned the right to be ridiculed by The Dean? What was the point? He would stop working as soon as Gordy turned his attentions to another student so why waste the tutelage on one so unworthy? Secretly Phil shared these same sentiments. Unsure though of a clear answer, Phil continued to subject himself to the Dean's emotional jabs. "Fat Phil that rope ain't tired. Pick it back up. Give that rope what it deserves now. Don't neglect him. He's more loyal that a Golden Retriever If you don't neglect him. Let's Go Philly. Up. Now." Phil would never be a contender. He would never be an amateur. He wasn't going to represent the gym or his city in a 10 round war. He would contribute no case studies to the sweet science. Gordy berated him still. He trained his emotions and his body still, knowing Phil would never even compete with anyone in the squared circle. Gordy simply wanted to see Phil compete with himself. "That's better Phil. Empty it out. Don't leave a drop. I want it all out. Focus on your breathing. I see you lying. Lying saying you're tired. It's a lie. Stop lying. This is truth serum time. That rope is infusing the truth all through you. Time!" Phil fell slowly to the floor as if it were a new mattress he wanted to lounge on for hours. He laid there breathing as if he'd come from the bottom of the ocean after being deprived too long of air. He laid there as close to exhausted as he had ever been. Yet he managed to smile. Time. Phil survived to hear the surrender of the enemy. He had defeated it. He had finally reached his *time*. He had never finished a full round of the ropes before. He looked at the dean for approval. Carefully as not to show joy, the dean kicked Phil in the sole of his shoe and leaned over to whisper to him. "And you're still alive. I can't believe it. Now we both know the truth. Don't ever come in here and lie again. Because now we know don't we...the truth. Hit the water fit...I mean fat Philly. Then get back to it"

This quiet and pure moment few had experienced. The Dean had whispered to Phil. The man was known for being smooth and sly with remarks. He had a stern charm with a boisterous humor in all situations in and out of the ring. His personality was of a leader that could control one million troops from facial expressions and ingenious charm alone. His whispers on the other hand represented an entirely different side of the man. His whispers came after his fast mind had input and downloaded new data to the file that was you. His whisper seemed to be to his students a succinct and concise report. It was a complete and thorough analysis of the subject. In his boxing gym it was revered as the most accurate of data output from one human to another. The whisper didn't lie to you. Gordy would only whisper a thing to you if he was of complete certainty of the matter. Phil knew he was never allowed to lie and omit truth in the gym again. He had been found out. There would now be new expectations he would be forced to live up to. The backside of truth is acquainted with brutality. Courageously Phil went on.

4

His Muse

He yearned for her in his sleep. His morning cardio sessions
were more intense on the mornings he knew he would see her.
He ate his favorite meals either with or directly after leaving
her. On this gorgeous spring evening she would taste like
lobster, taglioni noodles, pea soup and red wine. Always she
tasted like red fine wine. He overate with her joyously. Diet
be damned. The calories couldn't help but be burned in their
moments together. Colleagues took notice that he seemed to
be more attentive to minute details. He asked to be included in
email chains far below his station. He took delight in learning
more about operational activities of departments already well
managed. Through her eyes he was again falling in love with
the pieces that made up the puzzle. It showed in his leadership.
In the three quarters a failing wing of his business had been
pushed back into the black and he had successfully negotiated
an acquisition of an innovative bio science startup in Saint
Louis Missouri. The young company of course needing direct in
person guidance from him, forced him into multiple monthly
unavoidable business trips. Few people knew his truth. He

participated in multiple meetings with the startup, via video interface while still in the city at a quiet love nest he'd purchased for them. An 1100 square foot apartment with an office he designed to mirror that of his corporate location had become his sanctuary to her. There he mixed pleasure with business as she sat across the room silently mocking his serious facial expressions and tones. It had become a game to never show that there was such beauty so near him while he was engaged in battle. He lusted for her as she tried on different dress shirts of his in front of him. She would scoff at him before revealing a mischievous grin while listening to financiers complain of a lack of ROI so early in the process. She sparred for his attention at the very moments his legacy demanded his focus. Naysayers of multitasking had never practiced at such a level he had concluded. She knew when he was stressed. She would not allow him to explain his irritations until after she had emptied out his aggression and come up from her knees. What a counselor she was to be still so young. He had not raised his voice to a soul in three quarters. He smiled often now. She was his muse.

She loved her ability to override his rigid stern demeanor. She was able to paint now. Her vision for the not seen had been returned to her. She painted nightly and studied daily. There was no rule against waking up happy. Julia reveled in having no monotonous life mission thrust upon her. She painted. She smiled. She learned. He was the best teacher. Through his stories of business failings and legal interpretation she grew more aware of the world she had not been born into. She longed for his monologues that introduced her to reverse stock splits and debt obligations. She was fascinated by this new art that was corporate America. He enthralled her inquisitive nature with theoretical tactics of manipulating revenues through supply

23

and demand. He taught her. "Bug listen now. You are the consumer and are used to interacting with companies as such. There are some companies though that don't sell directly to you the consumer. They sell to other businesses. That's B to B love, as in business to business. Now this is what I want you to keep in your mind. Remember that every company has a product even if It wasn't sold directly to the public, or the consumer rather." He kissed her forehead as he continued. "Every company has a product. This too is true that, rather realized or not every person has a product. Wealthy people simply turned themselves *into* a product." She existed most in these moments with him. She had her professor all to herself. She swooned in his arms as she replied, "and what Solo is your product? What do you sell that I can get nowhere else?" She enjoyed irritating him only to bring him instant glee. She melted him at will. Life was good then. It was easier. Christopher Solomon, a 41 year old CEO of *Anima Corp* existed in a state of bliss. Julia kept him young. He was an adult man with a boyish crush on his lover. Even Julia was aware though; Anima Co. was his first crush. Stories of innovations from Anima Corp developed in him a constant thirst for knowledge and further wonderance. Since the age of 11 he read and studied everything about the way the behemoth constantly disrupted and the altered human experience. He had mapped out the first 50 years of his life and Anima saturated each step of his plan. He was blessed enough to grab the attention of its biotechnology Junior VP at the young age of 16 through emailing once a week with ideas, praise and questions on the *next big thing*. It wasn't until he mustered up the courage to offered critique of a quarterly earnings report that he received his first reply.

"To Mr. Gregerov,

Good afternoon again Sir. Its Christopher Solomon again, the high school sophomore that emails you relentlessly in efforts of gaining a prestigious mentor. My dad and I were exploring Anima's latest three earnings reports as well as its last four annual reports. I would greatly appreciate it if you would explain where the fire went. I have noticed that R & D spending has dropped dramatically in the last few years. Meanwhile Mr. Gregerov, the company's share prices have risen 64% in the same time period. This increase in stock price in my most humble outside looking in opinion, is a vote that you all will continue to change the world through innovation. I just don't understand how you intend to innovate if you guys refuse to spend the money you have? What is the point of the cash stockpile? Are we entering a war soon that few are aware of? Why not figure out how to grow re-generating oranges by next quarter or something? My dad tells me a wholehearted fail is indeed a win. Please don't start being fearful of failing just because you all haven't in so long. I also still would love to intern for you during the summer as I see now that my lack of failing is needed to revitalize the genome that is this miraculous organism that I intend to forever collaborate with, Anima Corp.

Always yours,

Christopher Solomon.

Without even a whisker on his chin, the kid really sent this email. Mr. Gregerov would read every email every morning and was not only familiar with the young students' emails, but rather looked forward to them. This time he felt the need to share with his peers the fact that his own logic pathway had true believers that would not be denied. He forwarded the email to the board members he was more friendly with. He forwarded it to his immediate staff as a reminder to never hold honest thoughts. He even forwarded the young man's email to the company's co founder and majority shareholder, engineer entrepreneur Adam Canon. Mr. Canon replied within hours. He was overjoyed that such a young focused hard working high school student had such strong interest in changing the world. He insisted his associate oblige the student with an internship and mentorship. "These are the people we hope to find out of Grad School. We instructed fate to bring us one of our own earlier than usual. This was meant to be Vitale. Bring him in. Teach him. Hopefully even learn from him." This began Christopher Solomon's path to disrupting the way humans existed. He had finally succeeded in Step one. Be co-parented and reared by Anima Corp. Running full speed through college and graduate school was a feat of ease for Christopher. He thirsted for his mentor's approvals. In 5 years Christopher had assisted the development of what he deemed the most exciting product since the home computer.

Christopher stood in his mentor's office beaming with joy. Mr. Gregerov was unable to contain his excitement. "The unlimited potential here has me astounded Christopher! This is most likely the most amazing discovery in my lifetime! This simply can not be real! If these data points are even mostly accurate, this innovation is the key to a second chance! This is quite phenomenal! It'll regenerate each cell in such short time!

Imagine being able to regrow entire forests that are stripped of resources in a matter of 8 months! I can not for the life of me believe such a small unknown entity in Missouri could come up with this! Solo my boy this is frightening and I love it for that reason. I feared your youth had overruled your reason when you demanded such a dramatic increase in the R & D budget. I'm so glad I ignored reason and pressed for the increase! Grand work acquiring this Jubilee so swiftly! Their work is quite extraordinary indeed. The feeling in my stomach right now is excitement and concern. How I have missed it so! This is... this is life 2.0." Christopher sat down as Vitale continued to gleefully examine the files Christopher had presented him with. Realizing Vitale would spend possibly hours in deep staunch investigatory paralysis he decided it best to depart. He thanked his longtime mentor for the words of confirmation. Solo glanced at the clock on Vitale's wall. For years the clock on Vitale's wall had such presence. Clocks existed to keep time. Christopher had always felt this clock dictated it. His scheduled departure time was in less than two hours. He rushed to his home to grab his prepacked belongings. He was once more summoned by necessity. The startup still in its infancy didn't require him this week. She required him. Julia had been without him for nearly a month. It was far too long.

Rushing out of the front door with his two bags, Christopher laughed as he recalled Vitale's failed attempts to insist he get an aide. At the very least an aide would have his luggage secured on the plane upon Christopher's arrival to the hangar. Christopher's true disdain with the idea of an aide revolved around sharing. He explained to Vitale he would need to share far too much in order for the aide to have any affect. "For this aide to actually aide me, I have to explain myself constantly. I would need to allow this person into my personal space far too often. I would need to ensure they possess the ability to not bother me for days at a time while still feeling involved. They wouldn't of course Vitale. You know this person would insist on offering to pick up dry cleaning or make dinner reservations or some other trivial exercise in an attempt to show loyalty and worth. My processes are my own. I do not desire nor do I have temperance to babysit a babysitter. I will continue to fly solo." Christopher's nickname was in fact Solo. Not only was Solo a shortened version of his last name but it also embodied his brain storming routines. Early on at Anima, he would contribute often to great discussions but only to the point where he reminded the team that he was one of them. The team would jokingly bet snacks on if an email would receive a response from Christopher or Solo. A reply from Solo had yet to be constructed with more than 26 words. Christopher was meagerly more eloquent averaging 34 words per response. For almost 7 months, the standing bet for a granola payout was a 19-22 word spread. The seasoned staff usually bet the under. His best work, or so he thought, came to him in seclusion with reruns of old TV shows playing in the background. For him certain shows were a familiar background noise that subconsciously had become an anchor as his mind drifted. Endless nights were spent hands wrapped, swinging on a heavy bag in his home gym while contemplating the manipulation of the compound structure of hard plastics. Up until he met her, he genuinely believed that no better way could a night be spent.

* * *

Rich smells infused the air of the apartment. She had cooked for him several courses. Her perfume teased his nostrils as he crossed the threshold. The wine glasses were chilled. From the kitchen Julia called for him. "Solo come here right now and look at this noodle on the wall! To the tooth!" He hugged her from behind as she pointed at her accomplishment. "This week al dente bug, next week two star chef for sure. I see nothing but upside from here." She looked at him smiling with her eyebrows raised and asked. "This is your attempt at sarcasm and charm isn't it Solo." His kiss to her forehead confirmed her assessment. Her reaction was an eye roll and a slap to his backside. She followed him through his every step through the apartment. As he prepared for a shower Julia leaned against the wall of the bathroom entrance. "Tell me every detail Solo. Tell me about the meetings and about what has you so excited this past month. I want to know everything. What color tie did you wear last Thursday. What did you and your mentor speak about. Leave out no detail! Where are you steering the ship to next?" Julia's interest for all things Christopher and Anima Co. never dissipated. She was as up to date as any Wall Street analyst could be on Anima. It was blissful how Christopher's two passions aligned so seamlessly. He spoke eagerly over the shower about the newest innovation and its world altering possibilities. She listened intently as he praised his mentor for going against his cautious default and aligning with him on the matter of increasing the research budget. Christopher's showers lasted ages when the topic became Anima Co., as it nearly always tended to do. The steamed covered glass door did nothing to hide the facial expressions she had come to memorize of him. Julia was so attached to Christopher that she was fully confident she could in that very moment draw with distinguished detail his current facial expressions of which she wasn't able to see.

29

His every motion with every correlating tone and innuendo was etched into her memory. It had become so that she could *hear* his face. As he turned the shower off and stepped out Julia stood there with the smile he yearned for from San Francisco. She tossed him a towel and asked, "

"So does this mean you will have to come back to sleepy St. Louis more? With all these big innovations and possibilities won't you have to put more attention into me? I mean of course into the new child this Jubilee." Christopher laughed knowing she had made no error. As far as Julia was concerned the St. Louis based startup Jubilee that gave Christopher reason to be away from headquarters so often was secondary. The time he spent with her was reason enough to leave California often and he would be better to never forget it. He assured her that his trips would not be infrequent as he truly did need to spend more time at Jubilee. The company had gone from promising to a force to be reckoned with in such a short time. He assured her also that she would never be neglected by him. She could never just as Anima could never be neglected by him. The three entities were far too intertwined, she, he and it.

"Bug tell me again, why you refuse to come with me back to California even for a week. We could spend so much more time together if you would." Christopher paused and scrunched his brow. He felt a pang in his stomach as he fidgeted with the wine glass. He mustered up the courage to ask Julia. "Is it...is there another man? You are not property that I own. You may not feel I have the right to know but damn it I need to know. I can handle it if there is another, but I won't be deceived. I must have the truth Bug. You never want to come back with me to California. Wouldn't the ocean inspire your art? I just don't understand. You want to spend so much time but decline the easiest solution

30

to achieve that goal. What else or who else is holding you here? Is that it? Is there someone else?" His eyes lowered as if to prepare for a striking blow.

Julia jumped from her seat and fell into his lap. She grabbed his chin to lift his face to hers. "Solo there can't be another. Even if I wanted there to be, it simply isn't possible. You are my story Solo. I swear it." She felt him take a deep breath. She studied his face. This was relief. She kissed him again to change once more his expression. Now he wore her favorite. His right eye winced and his smile slight but apparent brought her the most satisfaction. It was a far different smile than his eager one. This smile was that of an intense satisfaction. Julia had won again.

5

The Missouri Man

Standing before them with eyes closed, he began to speak slowly. "I tell you I could run the entire nation from right here in Missouri. The nation would be better for it too. We would be back to using common sense. God knows this nation needs common sense again. Humility too is needed. Humility on the world stage will strengthen ties abroad. My opponent lacks that humility. Running a nation is not a college football match. We need strength but we do not need false bravado. We should never again...after me of course, elect a man over 6 feet. For the sake of the nation, presidential height stops at 6 feet maximum!" The intimate crowd of roughly 1500 earnest supporters chuckled at their pick's stab at humor. Having gained the full attention of the group, Henry continued. "All jokes aside dear friends, we've lost something un-quantifiable. The world looks at America now as always for leadership. We are and have always been the innovators. This nation has led the way and I refuse to allow us to lose that. For some time though leadership has been inept and unsuited. These bumbling leaders assumed power under the auspices that our beautiful America could be run on auto pilot. Doesn't it seem to you that they think the winning is done by simply being here? When did the definition of progress change? When was it lessened?" From the group mutterings of agreement with Mr. Semita's sentiments could be heard. "America is a beacon for a reason. We innovate here. We create here. From here we fight evil. From here we press. From America we lead the world. America leads!" Filled with pride, the crowd cheered as Mr. Semita raised his left hand to calm them. "We've been so silly for so long. Choosing sides to agree with blindly? Acting like petulant children with one another because of small disagreements? America we CAN NOT lead with unrest among our own. There can be no more! Together Americans will be the guiding path for the World again! Together all of us will ensure that America leads! And it starts right here in my mighty Missouri!" The crowd erupted with cheers and chants of 'USA' as Tom, Mr. Semita's campaign manager hustled him off stage and into an awaiting SUV.

"That was great Henry! The internet will love this! We always get that grass roots feel that is nearly impossible to replicate when you come home. The nation loves the Missouri Man." Tom Ducomen chuckled before continuing. "You were starting though. I could sense it. I knew you were starting when I heard 'run the nation from Missouri'. You had about three more minutes but, what better to leave the crowd with right? I just fear somewhere in your incredible mind you truly believe that!" Henry, well aware of Tom's attempts to rile him, calmly responded, "Your east coast arrogance is showing again my friend. Your region has the history and the schools and many of the minds I'll give you that. You also have the hurricanes, the excessive wage disparity, ridiculous cost of living and, well... you're all jerks." Tom replied, "and when you win this election and relocate East for four to eight years, what do you think you will become? It is most inevitable my friend." The two men shared a chuckle as the neared Henry's Chesterfield home. "Tell me specifically why the nation genuinely couldn't be run from Saint Louis? I'm not suggesting a move of the nation's capital but if fortune 500 companies can be agile and adjust to a changing world through technology then so can government." Henry looked at Tom and raised his brow, as if to imply his move had been made in the never ceasing chess match of regional bias. "Henry, you can't be serious. There are multiple reasons that will never be possible. The main reason though is that if we really do get you elected, your cabinet would all resign if they had to come here throughout the year. Your brain trust loves summers in Maine and Martha's Vineyard. Their kids go to BYU and Princeton. The think tanks are on the East. And Hen, though you have the utmost faith in you Midwest salt of the Earth folk here, I doubt Farmer John fairs well as your Department of Agriculture Secretary just because he knows how to work his way around an unexpected frost." Henry lowered his brow and shared a light laugh with Tom as the SUV arrived in the driveway.

Henry Semita was 42 years old. He was independently wealthy. He had graduated with a Masters degree from Yale after attending Saint Louis University for undergrad in his native Saint Louis Missouri. In high school Henry triumphed in the chess club, he wrote debates for the debate team though he was not a member. He even wrote code for the school district to improve functionality for their online network. He was built for success. He was unable to accept anything less. While in undergrad he read about an engineer who was pushed out of his own company shortly after having it taken public. The engineer responded

34

by building several more. Henry was more than intrigued with this creator of the future than his trivial assigned studies. For years Henry seemed fixated on this figure. He felt compelled to interact with him. Henry arrived at the conclusion of the necessity of a detour. He was inexplicably meant to converse with the man, and so he did.

Adam Canon, now with a net worth of nearly 21.7 billion dollars, a reputation as a recluse and a clear calendar, had nothing but time to do what he believed he was intended to do. Build. Destroy. Research. Repeat. Feeling more than compelled to work in some capacity with Adam and with no other option, Henry decided to reach the billionaire via his public email which he was sure was never checked. He attempted contact still. Henry sent over 20 emails exuding reverence and desperation for a meeting. He lacked ability to truly formulate the words expressing what he desired to attain from Adam. He simply felt compelled. The emails would never receive a response until one day Henry read a personality trait article in which Adam had been profiled. Henry read this essay several times before sending his next email.

> "Mr. Canon,
>   "On 21 separate occasions I have failed to receive a response from you and I now know why."

He stopped typing. There was nothing more to say. Henry pressed send and continued his day. 19 days passed. On the 19th day Henry received an email that shocked him to his core. The email that would change Henry's future simply read, "Continue." In this moment Henry knew he had succeeded.

Every fiber in his being felt a satisfaction he was unaware he could feel. His calculations were correct. Now was the time to craft step two. Explain to a man, himself.

Henry explained to Adam Canon, Henry's understanding of him. He explained to Mr. Canon that he was never satisfied with discovering what had yet to be discovered. What he desired, was to define what had yet to be thought of. Any mere genius could stumble upon a finding. True meaning is in creation. Henry spoke on Adam Canon's feats at the helm of Anima. Henry went on to explain that Anima as well as any other project Mr. Canon took part of, were incubators of creation. Anima was not innovative it was motherly. A mother is well aware of what she will birth. The seed was strategized for. There was planning in the partnering and production of the offspring long before the seed began to grow. Adam Canon discovered nothing. He fathered. Henry sent this response to Mr. Canon and waited. He waited for nearly three months before he received a response.

Mr. Canon invited Mr. Semita to attend a dinner with him in California at his earliest convenience. He was told it would be quite alright to bring an associate with him. Henry elected to bring with him on this life changing event, his most trusted friend and business partner Tom Ducomen. Together they flew west, to interact with the unknown. Henry was then 31 years old.

6

Adoration

"You came Ness! Hey Come on let's get a drink." Mya greeted Vanessa as she entered the house party. Vanessa hadn't partied since she could remember. It would be good to be carefree for a few hours. Vanessa recognized one girl from high school named Elissa. Vanessa had been relatively close to her when they were younger. She waived at her from across the party. Elissa seemed happy to see Vanessa. She crossed the room to greet her. "Ness girl its good to see you out! I only really see you when I come back home from campus! How have you been? Are you still painting?" Vanessa shared with her some of her canvas victories as Elissa listened drinking the house punch mixed with vodka. It was good to catch up with one another. The cordial formalities lasted until Elissa noticed Mya coming toward them to interrupt the moment. "It was good to see you Ness. Hey give me your number, maybe you can visit campus with me one day. I'm going back over to my girls." They exchanged numbers as Mya approached. Vanessa noticed the tension between the two but decided not to inquire. "Mya." Elissa offered a lackluster smile in Mya's direction which Mya sarcastically returned. She then turned toward her friend. "Hey that dude over there was asking me if I knew you. Come on let's go talk to him." Vanessa saw no reason to turn down a reasonable request from her friend. Mya seemed to know 2 of the 3 men in the group. This put Vanessa's mind at ease. She wondered how long they had known her friend and why she had never mentioned them. Mya used to tell her about all her crushes when they were younger. The music was booming through the room and the party was crowded. He said he was unable to really hear her. He asked Vanessa to step away from the noise. She turned to let Mya know they would be in the front of the house but she and the other two men had gone. *'Some friend. Could have told me she was gone damn.'* Vanessa thought. He wanted to know what she did for a living. If she enjoyed it. What her plans were. He was interested in knowing where she was mentally and where she intended to be. He seemed to be fully engaged. After listening for so long and offering small insights on himself he decided she was perfect to share his thoughts with.

Of all the astounding matters the world offered to expound upon it was car insurance that they spoke on that summer night. "We all just need assurances in life. These insurance agencies know this. They know we will go through Hell to just feel assured. Most people never even have a car accident. Still we give them all this money month after month and for what? For a good feeling. What a joke." He spoke to Vanessa with such a sure energy. She drank and listened for a time before she replied, "Car insurance rates mean nothing to me sir. I don't drive." She chuckled as he rolled his eyes. "It's not about the car insurance really though. Its about the reason someone would continue to pay it after so many years of never using it. You know why they still do it? Because they want the feeling of security. Everybody wants to feel secure. We make those insurance companies rich so they can tell us they got us. Even if they don't. We should make each other rich like that. Secure each other. Doesn't that make more sense?" He leaned into Vanessa and asked, "You do see how we could all be self sufficient if we all just build each other up though right? Other communities do it so easily. We just need to sacrifice for a time and have follow through with a plan. We can change our own outcomes with no help." She loved his forward thinking. He and Vanessa had been standing outside for some time before she realized it was getting later in the night and the temperature was dropping. Vanessa turned to him to say her goodbyes. "It's getting late, and I have no clue where Mya went but I'll text you sometime though." He softly pinched the back of her arm as he spoke to her explaining that Mya had gone with his friends but was of course in good hands. He assured her he could get her home more comfortably and in far less time than the public bus ride she was so accustomed to. He wanted to continue to talk to her anyway this would allot more time to get to know one another. She at first refused, but he insisted that she wasn't able to inconvenience him. He just didn't want to leave her yet. The offer seemed reasonable enough. He told her he appreciated her time. He wished he didn't have to leave her. He leaned in and kissed her. Vanessa attributed his lack of passion to him being nervous though he showed no sign of fear. He told her he would love to be invited into her apartment. He simply couldn't dream of leaving her so soon. He offered a second kiss and assurance that whatever happened would be completely in her control. She obliged. And so it began.

The rain was warm and heavy. Vanessa was prepared. She was anxious to be home. She wanted to relax, draw and speak to him. Two days had passed since she invited him in. She missed him already. With her work shift nearing its end, her mind shifted to her voyage home. She knew at times when it was raining busses would drive through stops slightly faster. She had her belongings next to the counter. Two mere minutes lost could possibly delay the reunion with her bed and her by over an hour. She glanced up as she checked out the last two customers in line to see him. He stood in her line with random items pretending to have difficulty selecting between different candies and gums. As the last customer departed he placed several items on the counter and looked into Vanessa's eyes. She was powerless against preventing the smile she formed as he stood in front of her.

"These candies are 2 for 2.50$ right? I have 2.35$ Can we work something out?" He offered her a smirk as he pulled out a fresh 20$ bill. She told him how happy she was to see him. She asked him, "Why did you not tell me I would see you today? We have been texting all day why didn't you tell me you might come up here?" He replied he noticed it was raining and wouldn't have her in the rain at night so he decided to show up as he knew her schedule. He explained as she finished bagging his items. "I really didn't need anything from this store. I am only here for you. You and this deal on candy of course. I'll be outside when you lock up." This warmed her. He was considerate. He had come out in the rain for her. He cared. Could this be a new normal for her? Was this to be expected? Should she ask him what this meant? Did it mean anything? Was he just then thinking about her as she was him? Vanessa pondered these thoughts as she now calmly ended her duties. The need to rush had subsided. For the night at least, two minutes were able to be trivial as opposed to critical. What a feeling this was.

He drove Vanessa home in the rain while she rambled about

her day. As she spoke, she rubbed his forearm waiting for him to smile. He didn't but it was surely due to his need to focus on navigating the storm she concluded. She sat back in the seat and asked him how his day was. The response was blunt and lacking substance. Dissatisfied she continued. "Tell me what did you do today. I want to know every detail from the time you got up until this very moment." He shared with her the general outline of his day. He rose to run at 630 A.M. After his 3 miles he stretched, had a protein shake and napped. He told her of the errands he ran and the workout he had again by 1 P.M. He spoke to her about the boxing gym. He told her how he was undefeated and never intended to lose. He spoke on the boxing trainer that ran the gym. A man named Gordy who was hard to impress. Gordy wasted his time on the losers when he should be focused solely on him. He expressed his irritation with the lack of talent other fighters had. He had no respect for any of them. She listened as he expressed disdain for a fighter who he had never sparred with that seemed to be overly protected by Gordy. He voiced his frustration at the idea that Gordy protected the fellow fighter. Why did he deserve this? Was it because his father was in prison? Was it because he had chosen him to be the gym's prime pick? What made him deserving of so much specific tutelage? Vanessa had no time to contemplate a retort before he would continue. If the goal is to win and to make the gym a winner then protect no one. To protect a fighter is to offer that fighter a false sense of security. Furthermore what true fighter would want to be protected? A real fighter would want the biggest challenges. He and his fat friend made the gym weaker he explained. He as a part of this gym was made weaker by extension. How unacceptable it is to be susceptible to the flaws of another. She noticed the face he maintained while speaking of fighting. His nose scrunched his eyebrows low, with new lines in his forehead. His face expressed that he was fighting as he was speaking. This new energy from him Vanessa had yet to experience. He seemed to be in a daze as he spoke of fighting. She realized she was in the car alone. His body was next to her, but his mind was in the ring. He was fighting so he was gone. She attempted to get him back with a question. "Do you ever get tired from all of this?" The question seemed to break his trance. He looked at her as he pulled into her apartment parking lot. His response, a one worded low bellow of sorts startled Vanessa. "No."

* * *

As they restocked an aisle in the store, Mya listened intently to Vanessa's story of newfound lust and joy. Vanessa went on about how she loved the surprise appearances from him rather it be the apartment or there at the store. She loved the way she didn't have so many concerns when with him. She told her how he would pick her up nearly every night and take her home. She loved how available to her he was. "He stays with me so much I love having him there. It feels so much more secure Mya." Mya looked at her quickly smiled and turned back to her work. Just as if he knew he was being discussed he appeared in the store. Vanessa hugged him tightly. Mya released an uneasy smile toward him and continued to work. "Hey I'll be off in about 10 minutes!" He assured her per usual he would be outside and would pull up to the front when he saw her. Vanessa nudged Mya and expressed a wide smile as she gathered her belongings to leave for the day. She waived to her friend as she walked toward the door. As she left Mya called out to her. "Ness, just...enjoy the moments. Let those be enough OK?" Somewhat confused Vanessa replied with a nod and a smile. A tear formed in Mya's eye. She knew in that moment seeing her friend beam with joy that it was too late. Mya sat on the floor of the store and panged internally for what she had done.

"I know I said we'd see a movie today but I really need to get some work in. I want you to come to the gym with me. It shouldn't be too boring. Just give me a good hour and a half and then we can go." Vanessa grew excited. To see him in his element would be more entertaining than any film. She loved the idea that he wanted her to be in his comfort zone. She happily agreed to watch him train. They walked into one of the buildings but instead of going immediately to the gym, he told her he needed to speak with someone. She walked with him to the small eatery located within the premises. He told her to have a muffin or yogurt so she wouldn't be so hungry before the movie time. She sat in a booth with a yogurt and a bottle of water as she watched him sit in another booth with two men. He shook the hand of one of the men as the other man simply nodded at him. She watched them speak to each other calmly. He waived at her to let her know he wouldn't be much longer. She smiled and waived back. The two men looked at her as well and nodded their heads in acknowledgment of her. One of the men looked again at her and smiled and waived as he had waived. Blushingly she waived again. The man that did not waive excused himself from the table and walked out. A few people gathered around the man that departed as if to have reverence for him. He greeted them as he left. She watched as those same few noticed the man that her fighter was speaking to. She noticed they all went toward the booth to be acknowledged by him. He offered a halfhearted smile and continued with him. They spoke for several more

43

minutes before standing up to end the talks. Vanessa hurried her yogurt and grabbed her water as the man that had waived at her approached. "You are a beautiful one. Stick with this guy!" she smiled as she hugged onto him while the man departed. As they walked toward the gym entrance Vanessa said to him, "That man seemed nice. What does he do babe?" He pulled her into him as he replied to her. "He does a lot of things. What matters is what he'll do for us. He will open doors." She nodded in understanding as he opened the door for her. "I saw you give him your big smile too. I was jealous but I had to play it down." He laughed as he said to her not to share her perfect smile with anyone else. She laughed in response to his playful banter. As the elevator opened he grabbed her around her waist and looked deeply into her eyes. "Ness, don't share that smile with no one else but me. It's mine. I want it all to myself." He kissed her and pointed to a seating area in the gym for her. He was possessive over her. She loved it. The request was simple. Only smile for him. The offer seemed reasonable enough.

Vanessa watched other fighters greet him as he made his way to the locker room. A man handed him a jump rope and pointed toward a wall made of mirrors. She heard the man ask him if he was ready to work. He screamed back three words. "Built for it!" The man, a trainer Vanessa deduced, lightly slapped him on the back of the head and screamed back at him, "Protect the throne then Sultan!" Another fighter in the distance cheerfully screamed in his direction an affirmation. "Go to work champ! Protect the throne Pierre!" Vanessa sat and watched other fighters pausing to watch as he began his warm up routine with the jump rope. The gym belonged to all. The throne though, which stood for the gym's bragging rights, belonged solely to Pierre *The Prowler* Sultan. Vanessa watched him intently.

She saw his body seemed to awaken to the atmosphere. She noticed his ears move back as a trainer would give him advice. She noticed how effortlessly he threw combinations. He was a master in this world. Her eyes followed his every move. She wondered why he continued to look toward a middle aged man who was focusing on two other fighters across the room. She concluded he wanted this man's approval. Her face scrunched as she wondered how he had not yet attained it. After every exercise Pierre looked in this man's direction. He wanted to be rewarded with approval but found none. Another fighter asked the man, "Gordy would it have been wrong to side step early here knowing where the guy is going?" The man extended one arm to the young fighter's face to mirror a jab. She watched Pierre frown as he watched the head boxing coach Gordy teach the young fighter. "You threw a clean jab to make him move. So you know where he's going. He is going right where you told him to, right?" The young fighter nodded his head in agreement. Gordy continued. "So you can either meet him there with that right hook to the kidneys to slow his legs down or you can pivot and go for that knock out left hook to the jaw. But why are you pushing all your chips in on the first hand kid? He just showed you that if you lead he'll follow. So empty his pockets before you send him home. You understand me?" The fighter eagerly nodded and continued. Vanessa noticed that this coach Gordy was intentionally ignoring Pierre. She saw the frustration in his face as a different trainer told him to lock back in to the work. For several minutes he continued the drill. Shortly after two other faces walked past her and on toward the locker room. Vanessa noticed Gordy turn toward the two and say, "EJ go to work. Stay clear today. Control what you can and can not control. Figure it out. Wait just a minute! Fat Phil look at you man!

You're back again! I'm baffled. You know we still ain't having a barbecue after the training and you still came back. I love it! You might mess around and make winning a habit if you're not careful! You didn't bring a doctor's note or something to get out of this hard work did you?" As Phil sheepishly laughed and shook his head Vanessa noticed again as Gordy's face changed. He yelled out again to the pair. "Phil, get ready and get over here today. I'm in a torturing mood. You're with me first half of the workout." Astonished at the proclamation, Phillip rushed into the locker room as EJ walked behind him seemingly also quite surprised. Vanessa watched Pierre's face. His energy was different. She felt the change even from afar. He punched harder with each combination. She realized that now the pads on the trainer's hands he was punching had been replaced with the two faces Gordy had recently interacted with. A part of her enjoyed seeing genuine passion from him, though rooted in envy. She continued to study him. As he moved Vanessa wondered when she would be able to know his passion not in envy but in adoration...for no other subject than her.

7

H.E.R.

Tom awaited Henry in the lobby of the hotel. The two were off to visit a nearby Pennsylvania high school with a gifted robotics club. Henry noticing Tom's excitement inquired of his friend. "Tom you seem more anxious than usual. Missing your high school days? I'm sure security won't let you get hazed as much as you were your first go round." Tom laughingly replied to Henry that he was always excited to interact with the promising youth. "Hen these are the kids that will automate so much of human life. One of these very children could be the answer to ending war or improving deep ocean exploration. Their possibilities are endless!" Henry's eyebrows raised as he processed Tom's cheerful optimism. Henry, Tom and a few staffers walked through the school halls with the principal. They were accompanied by one of the leaders of the student robotics club. "Its so cool to meet you Mr. Semita. My name is Drew Xi sir and its so cool. I'm meeting the future president of the like whole country!" The adults laughed as Drew spoke zealously on how new ½ nanometer chips were the most important invention since electricity itself. Nearly skipping toward the robotics lab Drew went on, "Guys do you understand the immense capabilities of freaking 200 billion transistors! Like seriously the computing power can only be rivaled by the human mind itself! Now imagine us the human minds working in unison with this much capability! Everything alters from travel to entertainment. This definitely gets man to Saturn in like way less than 100 years!" Tom mouthed toward Henry the word Saturn as he chuckled at the teen's audacious dreams. Media staff snapped multiple photos of the student Drew and Candidate Semita entering the science lab where a select few students awaited. Tom watched intently as the students under their eager leader Drew, showed Henry multiple robotics designs and ideas. Tom smiled as Henry's eyebrows remained raised through each presentation. "Mr. Semita, wait stop everything dude. This is what you have to see now. You have to meet the HER." Tom stopped his side conversation when he overheard this request from the students. He joined Henry to see the creation the students were so eager to display. One student told Drew it wasn't nearly as good as he thought and shouldn't be what the future president was forced to see. Another student said Mr. Semita might find it weird or boring. Mr. Semita interjected. "You are presenting to us ideas. There is no such thing as an idea not being as good as one thinks. What ever this idea is, does it not as any idea would, instantly alter with each input? If then this is true can you all find it in yourselves to allow also mine? Let's meet this HER." Drew had heard enough. He sprinted to the back of the room and pushed out a table with an object covered. He and another student removed the covering. Some adults in the room giggled at what they viewed. There on the table sat what mostly resembled an upper torso of a woman with one arm attached. The figure was hairless.

48

Her eyes were a deep shade of blue with green. "This looks more like artwork than robotics kids." The principal remarked to the room. Henry's eyebrows remained raised as he walked around the creation. He turned to Tom who stood mouth agape. As he looked at his friend he asked the students what exactly HER was. "Well my older brother is on a robotics team at M.I... well a prestigious university. I send him every idea I have and one day he told me to stop having random ideas and start to formulate more focused ones. OK so fast forward to this girl I liked a long time ago in my freshman year. I wanted her to go to a dance with me but, like I'm realistic in some areas like girls, so of course no way. I said I needed the perfect date to make her furious with envy." The room laughed, all but Henry and Tom. Drew continued. "Well I got over the girl but not the idea of having the perfect date. Then I thought why not have the perfect everything? I told my brother we needed to build the perfect, responsive, functioning HER. A human like error less robot. Three years later we have...well we have HER." The principal smiled as if to take some form of credit for the student's effort. Henry, eyebrows still raised asked Drew, "What exactly does HER do Mr. Xi?" At once the entire robotics club began inaudibly exclaiming its capabilities and functions thus far. HER had learned chess and had not been defeated in 191 games. HER had been introduced to multiple books varying from 17th century European history to child psychology and development. "At this point HER is able to recall any information and answer questions about facts on demand. We are teaching HER now to dispute facts with previously attained information. Its going shockingly well. We expect that her will one day be able to..." Henry cut Drew's next sentence off and lowered his eyebrows. "One day HER will be able to argue. Meaning it will be able

to form its on opinion. It will be able to... to disagree." Drew
nodded solemnly. Tom lowered his head as if in deep thought.
He rose it to ask, "How exactly did you all do this? In a high
school with minimal supervision?" Drew explained he would
take HER to his brother's school and his friends would assist him
in programming and engineering. He would read and download
books to HER daily. Some of HER's code was open sourced even.
Tom's face froze. "You used open source code for this?" Drew
confirmed with one nod up and down and a smile. "Mr. Xi this
is extraordinary. One question. What purpose does HER fill?"
Another student stood next to Drew and spoke. "My dad was a
firefighter and he died when I was 8. They said he couldn't get
out of a burning house. His teammates did all they could to get
to him but they didn't find him in time. If HER had been fully
functional then, maybe an operator could have guided it through
the house with my dad. Maybe HER could have been in there
as a partner even. HER serves many purposes humans serve
Mr. Semita. Hopefully one day even saving lives." The crowd
clapped as one staffer hugged the young student. The cameras
continue to flash as drew proclaimed, "Worst case scenario
HER will always like my outfit and always want to play video
games with me!" The group laughed at the teen's attempt to
lighten his classmate's now solemn mood. Everyone shared
in the laugh, except Henry and Tom. Tom stared at HER and
frowned in bewilderment. Henry, brows raised, stared at Tom,
learning.

* * *

"This election should be a landslide yet somehow it isn't. This
young Black millionaire, running as an independent from the

middle of some farm somewhere in hills of Missouri still leads in several key demographics. We are 17 months out from election day and he is getting stronger. This is insane. How is this possible? He isn't old enough to lead the free world. What the heck is happening team?" Presidential candidate Bruce Stanfield sat glaring at his team of campaign strategists. Silence filled the room. Many at the table had an opinion but all lacked the courage to share. A staffer shifted uneasily in his seat. He froze instantly when Mr. Stanfield turned to him. "Ken you just volunteered yourself. Tell me how you're viewing this. How is he galvanizing so many groups that he shouldn't be able to?" The staffer cleared his throat as he timidly offered his assumption. "Well Mr. Stanfield. He's young enough to snatch the youth vote. He is an independent man. He has no kids no wife. It introduces a perception of a president's full focus being the nation solely. People like the idea that the president will belong to nothing but the cause. He has money, so successful people aren't afraid of him." Mr. Stanfield cut him off angrily. "That's ridiculous! I have money! My children are grown successful contributing adults! The fact that he has an empty bed should have people NOT trusting him! Why hasn't he shown himself to be loyal to one person? His lack of ties has him perceived as focused and available? Well we need to paint that as him being cavalier and reckless!" Several staffers jotted notations in notebooks and cell phones. Ken continued to address the room. "Well sir, I think the best thing you can do is show the groups we know you can't win, that they are indeed still your focus. This will in my opinion, show his supporters that he isn't much different than you. The biggest difference between you and he, needs to be his inexperience in government. Right now sir, that's a plus for him. If we can humanize you more to certain people though, we could make your experience work for you while simultaneously lessening this X factor he seems to bring."

Mr. Stanfield lowered his head to the table. As he rose, he locked eyes with the staffer across from him. He asked where she graduated from. She replied she attained her undergraduate degree from Northwestern. "Alright Emily from Northwestern, you're in. Whatever responsibilities Ken had are now yours." The room gasped as Mr. Stanfield continued. "Ken, explain to me you feeling the need to express that your opinion was indeed your opinion. It shows a lack of true belief. That screams to me, lack of assurance. Rather you were right or wrong you sounded weak. I have no room for weakness. I'm behind two touchdowns at home and you faltered when I called for the Hail Mary. We appreciate whatever you've contributed. Please slide Emily your credentials Ken and go off and find your damn voice or something. Keep the phone we'll write it off." Astonished and embarrassed Ken tossed his credentials into the middle of the table and stormed toward the exit. Before he walked out of the room he turned to the group. "The true reason Semita has such a grip on this election with no major party machine backing him is this. You are just another candidate. You are rich, old, White and not expected to bring any innovation to the world. The way you made your money was the old way. The way you ran your state was the old way. The way you operate is old. This is the time of electric cars, social media, talks of inner planetary travel and sharing of ideas with people you'll never meet online. Your ways are antiquated. They are dying and you show no intention of adapting. You still drive a damn beat up environmentally destructive diesel pickup on your property Mr. Stanfield and you are foolishly proud of it. You wonder why you are unable to get the chunks of the upper middle class vote?

It's because you're defiantly out of touch with the time you're in. Can you even set an alarm on your cell phone? Because the voters you can't seem to relate to can. They want to vote for the guy that they relate to. My God man you argued with your staff to also send faxed copies of emails when you ran for governor in your second term. Are you kidding me? You're already dead Mr. Stanfield, and you don't even know it." Mr. Stanfield offered a blank stare at Ken as he stood there waiting for the ferocious response. Mr. Stanfield calmly retorted toward Ken. "That sir is what you should have said the first time. All I am gathering is that you had a solution and were too timid to offer it in the time of need. Get out. Anyone else that is afraid to talk to me as an equal can leave with this sheepish man." Ken shook his head in disbelief and departed. Mr. Stanfield fidgeted with his already straightened tie and continued the meeting. Upon the meetings end he said only one sentence. "Fools can be corrected. I do not suffer cowards."

Presidential Candidate Bruce Stanfield was not afraid of a fight. He wasn't even afraid of losing. He was afraid of being perceived as noncompetitive. He competed at the highest levels since a child. He played the tight end and middle linebacker positions in high school football. He earned scholarships to play for Syracuse, Illinois, North Carolina, Baylor and Michigan State. He decided instead to play for Georgia. His collegiate athletic career would have ended of little substance but for one game in his junior year. His team was littered with injuries. Members of his coaching staff held audible disagreement as how to proceed in the second quarter. The team was unable to stop scoring in the first quarter and they were already down 21 to 0. Bruce knew he could at the very least slow the bleeding. He grabbed a defensive coordinator and pleaded to be subbed in. Before the coach could disagree Bruce slapped the coach on the shoulder and said, "You know this game is over if we don't hold that ball and give QB2 a fighting chance coach. I'm going in. Pretend it was your decision and make peace with it." He ran on the field for the first time in the season and immediately corrected his defenses stance. He demanded they narrow in. "Broken Arrow! Broken Arrow!" He screamed. One of the linemen began to show his concern for the plan but before he could do so, Bruce locked eyes with him and screamed. "I do not suffer cowards man. Arrow and do it now!" The opposing offense gained immediate confidence. They had just witnessed another player enter the game with no field time that season. The game was surely theirs. The opposing team snapped the ball and as their QB took his back steps, Bruce and a cornerback rushed from opposing sides. The opposing quarterback thought the defense was confused and thought it best to capitalize. He took one more back step when all of a sudden the same lineman that showed to be blitzing suddenly back peddled. Before the quarterback could realize he had thrown the ball into coverage, the linemen had intercepted the short 4 yard dump pass in the middle of the field. This was the most unlikely interception and left the opposing offense somewhat baffled. The linemen was brought down after fleeing just 4 yards. It was of no consequence. Mr. Stanfield had given his team another chance in the fight. Later in the second quarter Bruce was back on the field. He caused a strip fumble that he recovered. As he ran down the field he slowed. He saw the last man that could stand against him. It was the opposing quarterback. He slowed his pace to ensure the opposing offensive player had no choice but attempt to stop him. Bruce dropped his shoulder and plowed through the quarterback with as much power as he could muster. He ran the ball to a touchdown from a fumble recovery but his true intention was achieved. The crowd watched as the opposing team's star quarterback was carried off the field. Running back to his sideline he found the same defensive coach that hesitated to sub him in. "Thanks for believing in me coach." Bruce sarcastically remarked. His team went on to win the game by 3 points. He took this defiant win as a sign from the universe.

Bruce Stanfield would go on to found and acquire dozens of successful banks throughout the Southeast. He loaned to anyone with the desire to win, no matter the odds. His banks though would more than loan to the masses. He would partner with many small businesses that sought loans. He offered guidance and loyalty major corporations would never offer. Across the southeast, barring the poor souls unable to maintain interest payments on often conspicuously high loans, the back step sang Bruce Stanfield's praises. Anyone can say they want you to win. Mr. Stanfield is winning with us. He would be known as the banker that gave the second string a chance at a win. His popularity and successful track record allowed him to run for governor of Georgia and win by a landslide. That one college victory in his junior year was Bruce Stanfield's paradigm shift. He would live now by a new creed. Redirect the win toward you by punishing whoever it last favored. The opposition will lose their will to hold on to it. Then it is yours for the taking.

8

Monty

Vanessa stood behind the familiar store patron as he practiced his sacred lottery rituals. It was not until that moment that she realized she had not caught the bus since Pierre had entered her life. He was always available before she would even be able to need him. "Hey there Ness. Haven't seen you in a while." The store clerk Monty greeted Vanessa with a smile as she placed her items on the counter. He asked her how her art was going. She had not until that moment thought about art since the night she and Pierre spoke at the party. She pulled out her phone to show Monty the last two pieces she started months ago. He implored her to keep it up. He reminded her of the painting she made a year ago and how beautiful it was. As she searched in her phone gallery for it, the door to the store swung open. Pierre entered with a frown. Monty greeted him and continued on with Vanessa until Pierre walked to the counter and snatched her phone. His face riddled with irritation, Pierre angrily interrogated Vanessa. "What are you doing in here girl? You know I'm sitting outside and you're in here showing pictures to this dude? What is this? You can't be serious!" Shocked at his level of anger, Vanessa grabbed his index finger and attempted to explain she was engaged in nothing more than harmless conversation. "Babe I've been showing Monty my art since the 8th grade. It isn't anything crazy. Calm down please." Instantly she knew she had made an error with him. Standing at the counter she saw his light dim. His ears went back as if he had heard a command. Standing there Pierre seemed to look through her. Sensing the misplaced tension, Monty interjected. "What's going on bro. Ness has been coming here for years. My wife and I knew her mom and know her well. She means no harm young blood. Just looking at that art she makes. Hear I'll finish ringing you out Ness. By the way I'm Monty what did you say your name was again my man?" Without shifting his eyes away from Vanessa standing before him, Pierre responded in a low tone, "I didn't." Still looking at Vanessa he continued. "It's time to get up out of here Ness we got other things to do." Unable to hide her discomfort or embarrassment Vanessa gathered her items and turned to Monty. "Hey thanks again tell your wife I said hey. I'll finish those art pieces eventually." Monty nodded his head as he stared intently at the side of Pierre's face. Disapproval of Vanessa's public embarrassment showed in Monty's eyes. "Come on Pierre I didn't mean to take so long we can go." Watching the two leave the store Monty realized that name was for some reason familiar.

As the day progressed, he tried to no avail to recall hearing that name and in what context. As he decided to move on with his thoughts, a customer placed items to be purchased on the counter. "Sir you got yourself two cases of beer, 3 bags of chips, 2 decks of cards, 3 packs of candies, a bottle of Vodka..." Monty Suddenly stopped abruptly. The sight of the playing cards jarred Monty's memory. He remembered the friend's party...the card games...the two women...Pierre. The store now closed for the night, Monty sat quietly to recall a night he had blocked out for so long.

* * *

"My main man Monty! Good looking out on the discounted drinks my guy! Even though you're probably going to drink all the good stuff yourself!" Monty laughed as he greeted his old friend Chuck. The hotel suite was a nice accommodation he was able to attain at a discount through his employment. It was the perfect spot for hours of poker with old friends. "I never thought I would see the day our main man Byron got hitched. I thought he'd play the game til he checked out!" The two laughed as they exited the elevator toward the hotel suite. Monty asked Chuck, "Who all is coming through C?" Chuck responded to Monty it was the usual friends and possibly a few fresh faces. As the night progressed Monty noticed Chuck and Byron repeatedly looking at the door and checking their cell phones. He wondered, had they ordered food? Were they assuming more people would come? Monty skipped a round of poker to use the restroom. While away, he overheard Chuck, "Finally you made it. How are you ladies doing? Make yourselves comfortable ladies. Whatever we have to drink you all can help yourselves to." Monty washed his hands and emerged from the bathroom to see two younger females, neither older than their very early twenties, possibly younger. One of them poured herself a drink as the other woman sat to herself. Byron hugged the woman that had helped herself to the refreshments. Monty watched as he asked her, "What's up with your friend? Why is she all off to herself like that?" The woman playfully responded that she was fine and just needed to be warmed up to the group. Monty looked toward the suite door. He watched Chuck speaking with a male in the doorway in a low tone. He couldn't quite see the man's face but he was able to overhear small pieces of the conversation. "No not at all, I guarantee he'll enjoy himself. You just text me at this number directly. Nope you don't have any concerns like that at all. Those two are both perfect. Have a good time. You have zero concern. Enjoy the party for me too." Monty could see Chuck shake hands with the figure on the other side of the door before he closed it.

"Ladies this is my real good friend Byron. He is walking the plank next week to the point of no return. We just don't want him to go into marriage too hungry." Monty still confused stared at Byron hugging the woman that was drinking. He noticed then the other, quiet woman. She was visibly uncom-fortable. He asked if she was OK to be here. Without looking at him she replied she was. He said there was some snacks and bottled water she could help herself. The young lady shook her head in appreciation. Monty had seen enough. He pulled Chuck to the side. "Dude what is this?" Chuck with a drink in one hand explained that Byron just needed a proper send off before marriage. The women were there simply to have a good time and party with them. Monty was not satisfied. He asked who the man at the door was. Chuck simply replied he was their ride. Monty dropped his head in disappointment. He knew his old friend was lying to his face. As he continued to question Chuck, he noticed Byron and the woman that was drinking laughing in the corner. He then overheard him say, "I want her though." The quiet woman that was seated, looked up. Monty could see the uneasiness in her face. She managed to offer a slight smile. Byron walked over to her and held out his hand to guide her to a separate room in the suite. The woman looked back at Monty as she disappeared with the drunk fiancé. Monty was stunned. He refused to hear Chuck any further. He rushed to gather his belongings with anger in his face. Chuck attempted to calm his old friend. "Monty man you are really overreacting its not that deep man. Its all in good fun." Monty stopped long enough to look his old friend in the eye and ask, "How's Elisa doing at school C? Your niece is nearly their age on a college dorm. I dare you to call her tonight and make sure she isn't in any kind of situations tonight that some man would just write off as 'all in good fun' brother." Monty stormed out of the suite angrily, pushing past Chuck. He was too angry to wait on the elevator. He needed to be in motion. He ran down the steps toward the parking lot. Monty was nearly home when and somewhat more calm when he decided to call his wife. He could not wait to be home and forget about the night. He would first see if she wanted anything to eat. Patting his pockets and looking in his jacket he was unable to locate his phone. At a red light he recalled his steps and it hit him. The cell phone was on the poker table when he spoke with the young woman that seemed uncomfortable. He had to go back.

Monty knocked several times on the door before Chuck answered it. Standing in the doorway he could tell something was not right. Chuck was uncomfortable and uneasy. "You forgot your phone it was on the table. I'll get it wait here." Monty didn't respond. He was somewhat concerned as to why Chuck's face was flush with discomfort. Standing there he noticed the music was no longer playing in the suite. Monty could take no more. He stepped in to the doorway. The few party goers had gone. Byron sat on the couch with his head low. Chuck turned to see Monty in the doorway staring at him. The woman Byron had decided against sat near him on the couch with a blank stare on her face. All of them listened to girl's cries. One man stood outside the doorway to the bedroom. Through the cries and please Monty managed to overhear the young woman cry out, "Pierre please!" From the room there was a long pause then a continuance of cries. Monty glared at Chuck angrily. Chuck sheepishly looked to the floor. Compelled to stop this evil, Monty reluctantly made a decision to intervene. As Monty walked toward the man guarding the door in attempts to stop the attack, the man pushed his jacket back to show a silver 9 millimeter pistol. There would be no intervention. Monty grabbed his phone from the table. He stood within inches of Chuck's face in anger. He would not allow Chuck to simply look at the floor and fake innocence. Monty stood directly in front of Chuck for what seemed like an eternity as all listened to the young woman's pleas fade. She had given up. The voice of the man screamed at her. "You need to stop crying and get dressed Mya! Hurry up!" Monty could withstand no more. Perplexed and disturbed, he fled the hotel and headed home to his wife. He decided he would burden her with the night's events.

The memory stuck with him now. He was again haunted by what he previously suppressed. He was vexed once again by the two words. "Pierre please." Monty felt pain in his chest as he realized that it must be him. As he locked the door to the store a memory of Vanessa's first paintings crossed his mind. She was a kind and innocent young woman. She had no clue she had entered into a bond with the bond-less. She didn't deserve her impending doom. It was in this moment Monty performed the act that enabled all men throughout history to change the world. His brow lowered. He grit his teeth. He took one deep breath and it was done. Monty had made a decision.

61

9

Not Gods

"You feed me too much Bug. Look at my shirts. They are snug on me now. I need you to mock and ridicule me. Nope, don't look away woman. Look at this!" Christopher grabbed his own side and pulled. He was exaggerating his issue but he had indeed gained 6 pounds in the last 3 months. As he packed a bag for the gym Julia sat on the side of the bed and watched him. He was irritated with his happy weight gain. Julia loved it. "The more fat I get you the less women will want you. Now you're leaving me to go work against my master plan. Solo you make me sick. Stay and drink wine. Be who you are my love." He laughed hardily at her request as he finished packing his bag. "You're going to that gym that those young entrepreneurs built? The ones that started Jubilee?" Christopher confirmed with a nod and a kiss to her forehead.

He needed to speak with Ralph Mitchell on business matters and decided it best to do so after a good workout. He assured Julia he would be back in a matter of hours. "You're welcome to come Bug. You might have fun. I can teach you how to throw the proper uppercut." Christopher started to shadow box in front of her as she heckled him. "You're a bum fighter! Get out of the ring! Go home to your amazing girlfriend you bum!" Christopher released a boisterous laugh, hugged Julia and left for the Lair. Julia sat on the edge of the bed for a time. She went to where she kept her supplies and began to sketch. She was unsure what she was seeing but still she drew. As she sketched, she contemplated Christopher's daily routine when he was away in California. She longed to go back with him. She knew though the risk was too high. Being so close to Christopher was risk enough. Best to not tempt fate nor override probability.

Her abstract sketch brought to her certain memories. She recalled the rooms. She first felt cold in of of the rooms. She remembered shivering. As she sketched she remembered sitting cold and confused staring at the one way mirror in one of the rooms. She remembered shivering and waiting as she could only watch the breath from her mouth. For what seemed like an eternity she sat in the room quiet, alone and cold. Julia would never risk being subjected to those rooms again. She would destroy herself before she would ever be his experiment again. She sketched and recalled. She remembered his voice asking trivial questions for hours on end. "Who am I? What did you eat this morning? Who am I? What state are you in? In what country is California? Who am I? What did you eat this morning? Did you enjoy the food? Where were you born? Who am I? Who are you? Are you sure?" She quickly comprehended the true intention of the line of questioning. He wanted to see her compute the responses in real time. Her sketching stopped. She wanted to remember no more for a while. She was now years removed from the rooms but could still recall when she created her art. She placed the sketch in her folder and decided to change her day's activity. She could comfortably process no more memories. Her art would again be a necessary casualty. Memories of the rooms, of his voice and of California were to be suppressed at least for the day.

* * *

Christopher warmed up with jumping rope 1 minute without cease. He repeated it 3 times. He was warm now. He moved on to crunches and leg raises. He felt tension and tightness in his core and lower body. He had strayed too long. He was quietly ashamed. The lair though was perfect punishment for his gluttonous sins. As he worked through his processes, he noticed a young man jumping rope in the mirror under the watchful eye of what Christopher perceived to be his friend. He overheard the friend say, "Keeping going Phil 20 seconds." Christopher smiled to himself. He admired their teamwork. As Phil finished his routine, Christopher watched on as the friend bumped fists with him. "EJ man I'll be borrowing your tiny t shirts soon my guy. Just wait!" Christopher couldn't help but laugh to himself. The young man Phillip was demanding a different reality form himself. Christopher respected it. After a time of crunches and stretches Christopher made his way to one of the heavy bags across the gym. As he went through several combinations he watched the young friend EJ shadow boxing. He noticed how natural his movements were. His cross arrived right before a hook as a tsunami follows an earthquake.

The shadow boxing was interrupted as the main boxing trainer Gordy approached EJ. Christopher watched as EJ's excitement grew from whatever news Gordy had just delivered. He and his light footed friend Phil high fived and threw punch com-

64

binations into the air. Gordy slapped EJ on the back of the back and told him loudly to be prepared mentally. As Gordy walked in Christopher's direction, he stopped him to ask about the interaction. "What's that kid so happy about?" Gordy explained that he would be in an upcoming bout with another boxer from a Colorado gym within the next eight weeks. "Is this kid EJ a good fighter? Can he win?" Gordy smirked as he responded that if he could maintain mental discipline in all moments, he could run through a weight division. Surprised Christopher thanked Gordy and continued working. Before moving on Gordy took Christopher's hands and put his right fist lower. "You're a righty. We know it, but you still ain't gotta tell everybody. A man has secrets Mr. Solomon. Throw it after you throw two lefts back to back. By the way, heck of a quarter up at Anima again. You guys are always unpredictable yeah? Well, be unpredictable in this kind of fight too. I want to see two junk mail lefts sent before the right that you keep sending first class mail." Christopher grinned and nodded his head in confirmation. Gordy stood a minute longer to ensure his demands were meant. "Much better Solo. Keep doing it though until its natural. When you eat, sometimes use your left to hold the fork. It helps the brain remember that both sides of the body are equal. Keep at it man and speed it up a bit." Christopher nodded again before Gordy left his last remark. "Yo, last thing. I don't know what the hell you're doing in those gyms out in Cali, these STL eyes are telling me you're getting fat. My wife tried to do that to me. Don't let it happen. Whoever she is, tell her stop feeding you so damn much Mr. Solomon." The two burst out laughing before Gordy finished with a serious face. Christopher had received the confirmation that he was indeed being steered toward a gargantuan existence. Julia would have to hear of this immediately when he returned home. He threw his combinations leading and ending with the left.

As Christopher and EJ put back their gloves, Christopher spoke to the young fighter. "Hey, congrats on your upcoming fight dude. You ready for him?" Excited to discuss the upcoming bout, EJ turned to Christopher to explain in detail how well he would dismantle his opponent. Phil interjected that if any of the opponent's team members were to jump in the room that he would be the first to jump off the turnbuckle to defend his dear friend. Phil added something that would immediately resonate with Solo. "You're a fool to not expect someone to not break a rule to win a war." As Christopher departed to meet with Ralph Mitchell, he asked the pair what they did for a living. EJ replied, "We're on the janitorial staff with the Anima labs and offices here in St. Louis. It's a Pretty OK gig for now." Christopher grinned and retorted, "Yeah it's a great company isn't it? By the way guys my names Christopher but people close to me call me Solo."

Chipper Harris Mason and Ralph Mitchell sat at a table with Christopher in one of the rooms designed on the campus Chipper had built. Chips pulled up a document on his laptop as Ralph pulled out a tablet while Christopher spoke. The two wanted to speak further with Christopher on how best to utilize Jubilee's newest discovery. The team at Jubilee were sure they had constructed replicable cell re-stimulation. "Mr. Solomon I can understand the need for profit of course. I know we have to concern ourselves with shareholder interest now. I just know this is so much bigger than those trivial things sir. We can regrow what we have been destroying. I admit, I have been daydreaming about un-endangering species." The three men laughed as Chips continued. "This has to become a product we are aware. Ralph wont let me forget this vital point. I simply want to ensure this is much more. We have grown vegetation. I even tasted one of the oranges we produced. It was perfect. We need to accept that it is time to attempt regeneration somewhere in a desert. We can alter." Ralph cut Chips off and pounded his fist once on the table. "My good friend doesn't agree with me quite yet but he will once he sees. Its time to start human testing. We know we can grow vegetation. We may very well be able to fight carbon pollution with this. The true majesty of this though are our soldiers Solo. Every week we play around with the truth is a week wasted. And what is the truth? The truth is we more than likely can replicate lost limbs for our wounded. We can more than likely recreate organs that are damaged due to illnesses. We are sitting here talking about oranges when we should be having our labs exploring on the reattaching feet for diabetics. We could be months away from curing comas. Screw oranges. We need to be running full speed ahead."

Christopher took a deep breath. Noticing the concern in Chips face, he turned to him. "Chipper, why are you not fully on board with going in this direction? What scares you?" Chips closed his computer. He looked up toward the ceiling before addressing the two.

"Gentlemen we are smart. We are able to create. We can contribute to changing the world. We have all made millions of dollars. We have most definitely enriched the lives of millions through our endeavors. We are powerful men. But that's all we are...men. We are not Gods. And we are not God. Ralph are you not of this school of thought? If the U.S. or any government were to provide to every citizen free housing and free food, it would remove all desire to strive for more? If a man knows his mishaps can be erased, would not that man become reckless and in turn a danger to those around him? Would not the nation be overloaded with unwanted babies if zero people were afraid of STDs and everyone stopped using condoms? The fear of STDs causes people to take precautions that in turn prevent tens of thousands of unwanted pregnancies. This same logic gentlemen is applicable. Many people would live a far less healthy life if they knew a new liver could be procured upon request. I don't mean to argue a counterfactual but..."

Ralph interrupted Chipper to add, "but you did Chips. You did argue a counterfactual. Your entire argument is constructed on not only worse case scenarios, but... Jesus Chips. Why do you have no faith in the same humanity you claim to want to aide? This isn't as parallel to free food as one might think. Furthermore of course there would be barriers to obtaining these fictitious organs and limbs. Authorizations and narrative would of course be put into play Chips." Upon hearing this Chips' anger rose. He stood up from his seat and yelled. "Oh? So basically instead of restoring the Earth and feeding nations, we need to ensure the wealthy have access to new hearts? You want to take this miracle and sell it to the highest bidder? This will not be wasted to under gird the RNA of the wealthy. This will only further healthcare inequality! Now the wealthy will live longer and longer, possibly literally forever. What does that do to the already under insured. Jubilee will not construct a healthcare caste system!"

Christopher rose his hands up toward Ralph and Chips to calm the conversation. "Guys. You both make incredibly valid points. I must say our video calls are never this spirited and this proves I must fly out more." Seeing his attempts at humor fail, Solo continued. "We operate in a free market. We also have a duty to do what is best for the world. We will do well and do

68

good. Ralph, I see your vision. We could be only a matter of years away from unprecedented life saving procedures. Chips I also see your concern. You are not wrong. As all resources do, regenerated organ procedures would go toward the wealth almost exclusively. Guys the solution wont be found tonight. We aren't even still outlining the issues. I leave both of you with two separate questions. Chips, if we are able to do a thing do we not have a responsibility to do so? If we are able to create good, would disproportion be reason enough to not? Ralph, would you still want to push trials of human organ regeneration further if governments outlawed the use of our sciences to do so for profit? If only soldiers and citizens on wait lists were to receive these miracles would you lobby as intensely? I want not only our Jubilee to thrive financially, not only to innovate, but to be a pure entity. This may sound silly, but I want Jubilee to remain as wholesome and forthright as possible. We must raise this child with integrity because she will hold immense power. We'll talk more soon guys." Christopher shook the hands of Chipper and Ralph. He felt a sense of accomplishment after the meeting. The next steps for jubilee's discovery hadn't been decided but he was able to once again confirm Anima had made the right choice to acquire Jubilee. Its founders had passion for the direction of their child. This pleased Christopher. He left the campus to head to his apartment, and back to Julia.

10

St. Louis Connections

Phil swiped his badge to enter the break room where he knew his friends awaited him. "Let's see it man. It better look green healthy and leafy bro." EJ and two others waited for Phil to seat himself. They were all anxious to see his lunch choice. Phillip had eaten healthy for 11 days straight. He hadn't even taken his earned cheat meal day. His crew now wagered on how many days he could manage to stay away from the higher calorie delicacies. "Man 11 days and you're still at it P. That is really good man. Honestly at this point, whenever you stop you have earned it. It's all bonus time at this point." Phil uneasily accepted his friends attempt at encouragement. EJ didn't seem to realize that Phil no longer wanted pretty good. He wanted to be as great as possible. He didn't want people to expect him to cave under pressure. His wants had changed. He wanted to win and would by extension choose to want whatever enabled winning. For now, it was green leafy veggies and chicken breast. "If I shut my eyes super tight and just reminisce, this taste like the best of every fried food ever. I mean fried anything, fried shrimp, fried rice, fried whole grain wheat bread, fried oatmeal. I swear I don't even care at this point guys." The group laughed as other Anima employees entered the break room. EJ and Phil had worked together as custodians at Anima Corp since before graduating high school. EJ would train after school and Phil would join unless his desire to play video games was more insatiable than his desire for punishment. The two had been friends since the 7th grade when Phil shared with EJ half of his lunch. EJ respected his willingness to sacrifice half of his sandwich and snack cake and so their great friendship was forged. Eventually Phil would convince Eric to game with him. Eric agreed but on two conditions. "Phil if I start playing these video games then you have to start working out. We go hard five days a week in this gym and we game two days a week. Those are my conditions. Do you agree to these terms man?" Phil agreed to Eric's terms assuming Eric's sincerity would eventually waiver. It never did. As much as Phil would attempt to hate the consistency of his friends demands, he could not help but notice that... he was changing. When Phil first entered The Lair he could hardly move his body without pause. Now he was able to jump, sprint and shadow box at the very least with no fear of embarrassment from fainting. Eric would not complain. He praised any sign of progress shown. "When I log on, I'll send you a message P. I'm sure my system has to update first." Phil, Eric and others would often play certain games in team mode online. The game system offered multiple methods of communication. When one of the teammates appeared online he would be able to leave either a voice note or text note to another teammate. Eric would learn quickly how to use the system. They spent hours when not in training, in groups online. "Press that middle button EJ and then you can just type out a message and it will go privately to me. The rest of the team can not see it. It's pretty much free text messaging from system to system." Eric was impressed by the gaming system's capabilities. The online community had a way to speak shorthand through messaging as to not waste precious seconds between matches. One would need that time for restroom relief and snack replenishment. "Phil I cant even lie man. I see how this kept you fat. This is wild P." The two laughed over the headset as they invited others into their private team chat. Before opening access to the chat Phil reminded EJ, "OK its running. Switch to game names." Phil had showed Eric that no gamer used their real first or last name. Most gamers wouldn't even use publicly known nicknames. Eric responded as the chat filled with teammates. "Gotcha *Doublethreat.*" Upon understanding and accepting the gaming culture Eric would go on to utilize the gamer tag '*Heavyhand*' as only a fighter should.

* * *

Gordy stood in a corner meticulously examining every aspect of EJ's movements. In a fight, adjustments are made from rigorous repetition. The alternative is to adjust instinctively. One might see little harm in relying even lightly on instinct. Surely the human brain knows to avoid danger? Surely man is able to escape impending doom? How could instinct be the fatal flaw during such a period of structured intensity? The answer found EJ often in bouts. "The issue with you moving off of your instinct is this. You start off utilizing instinct. As the fight progresses those instincts turn into emotions and irritations. Your decision making should at all times be based in clarity and training. This is not basketball. You try new moves on this court and the hard foul will be life altering. Do you understand me Eric?"

EJ and Phil continued to work and train. Gordy was pleased with EJ's consistency in sparring. He had only lost focus two times in over 4 sparring sessions. A dramatic improvement. Gordy watched as EJ and Phil did their crunches and leg raises. His attention was interrupted by another trainer speaking to him in a low tone. "They are adamant on the fight. They want him. He's always prepared Gordy. This fight has to happen. We may as well put it on the same night as the kid here." Gordy rolled his eyes. He knew his assistant was correct. He knew Pierre was more than prepared. He simply didn't want him sharing a card with EJ. But it had become unavoidable. A gym in Chicago had an undefeated fighter and they wanted to test him against the best in Gordy's lair. They were aware of Pierre's pristine fighting ability and felt he was the only realistic opponent for their future star. Gordy told the assistant trainer to accept the fight and have it on the same card as EJ's fight against Hernandez. He knew as he gave this command what the question would be. The assistant asked as expected. "So who headlines this thing now?" Gordy looked in his direction and away again. His response was short. "Decisions need to be made. And they will be."

Gordy told EJ and Phil to hang it up for the day. He told EJ his training would be altered starting tomorrow. "Hydrate and keep the nutrients up. Clean eating only now. Phil keep him in line." EJ chuckled. Phil did not. He agreed to keep his friend on track as much as possible. As the two entered the locker room they saw a familiar face. "Hey guys how's the training going?" EJ and Phil offered a fist bump to Christopher Solomon. They each told him of their day's routine. EJ shared the date for the fight and said he planned to dominate his opponent within 3 rounds. "Hey I should be back in town then. I'll try and come! You better be ready the company will disown you if you get thrashed too badly in there." EJ and Phil looked at each other in confusion. "The company?" Phil replied. Christopher laughed as he told EJ to search his name and bio. The two looked at the phone and both busted out in laughter. "Are you serious dude? That's wild! We totally should know that right? I absolutely should have known that! You have to be on the wall somewhere in the building!" The three of them laughed. Phil asked what he was doing in St. Louis so often. Christopher explained the Jubilee acquisition required hands on oversight often and that he just had come to love the town. "Hey, you should have us be your St. Louis Connections. When you don't want to fly all the way out we can act on your behalf like your STL consiglieres. If you need something here while you're away, we come in, and we make em an offer they can't refuse." Phil put the tips of his fingers together and shook his hand to impersonate the gesture seen in Mob movies. Christopher chuckled and mimicked the gesture back to the pair. "One day I may call on you. Stay close."

The three of them shared a laugh. Phil offered the CEO his information in order to join them in a grueling workout when in town. Solo, remembering how rotund he'd felt in the previous months agreed the idea might be warranted. He gave the pair his personal cell phone # and told them to stay focused on the training before departing the lair. Phil turned to EJ. "You think he'll let us use him as a reference on resumes?" EJ shoved Phil playfully as they left to begin their night's video game session.

11

True Jubilee

"This is the third damn time it hasn't started in the last week. I'm sorry Ness." Pierre popped the hood of his car and raised it. His perplexed look caused Vanessa to hug him around his waist. "It's not your fault. Things break down. Does it need gas?" He shook his head and replied the tank was over half full. Vanessa hated that she was powerless to help him. No one stopped as he waived his hand for assistance. Pierre slammed the car door and sat on the hood with jumper cables in hand. Vanessa sat next to him and rubbed his back. "I need this car to last while I get just a few more fights. They have me on a new training regimen and I needed to be there super early. What if no one is around to give me a jump when I need to be at the gym? 4 more fights and I can buy a new one. But if my training slacks it's all over. Damn it what kind of luck is that?" As he continued to attempt to flag down assistance, Vanessa grabbed his arm. "Would $1,000 help? I been saving it forever but if it can get this car to make it for four more fights then you can just pay me back! That way you won't miss training." Pierre turned to her surprised at the idea. They spent most days together or speaking, and never had she mentioned the savings. "I don't feel comfortable asking you to help me with this. Are you sure its OK Ness?" She assured him she was fully onboard. He agreed that she would be paid back in full as soon as he could do so. The deal was sealed with a kiss. Finally, a driver pulled over and offered assistance. Vanessa returned to the passenger seat as Pierre and the stranger jump started the car. She felt a sense of relief when it started instantly. Pierre thanked the man again and put the car in drive. "OK first thing after training tomorrow while you're at work I'll go get the car worked on. Some patch work repairs should keep it going through four more fights. See I told you when I met you that we could build each other up and change our own outcomes!" He kissed her hand as they proceeded toward her apartment for the night.

The next day at work a manager asked Vanessa if she had heard from her friend Mya. The question surprised Vanessa as she came to the realization that the two had not shared a text in over a week. "Well, I know the last time she didn't work for a full week it was because she had pneumonia. I'll text her today and let you know what I find." The only time Mya was absent for such a long period of time was a little over a year ago. Vanessa remembered receiving a text from Mya at 4:30 AM telling her to let management know she wouldn't be in because she was bed ridden. Vanessa, concerned for her friend elected to bring her soup and supplies even while on the bus, but Mya would not allow a visit. She texted back she would bare no visitors while she was sick...for fear of the spread of her illness. Vanessa agreed to stay away so long as Mya sent a daily text with updates on her condition. Vanessa remembers texting Mya that evening, "You better keep me updated. We have to look out for each other out here LOL." Vanessa recalled not receiving a text back until the next day. Mya had simply responded, "Right. TTYL." Vanessa attributed it to a weary spirit. Illness tends to bring that about.

"If she's sick again I'll try to pick up some of her shifts that we don't already overlap." The manager thanked Vanessa and walked to the back of the store. Vanessa texted Mya two times during her shift and once when she was about to leave for the day. Her concern grew as she received no response.

Pierre arrived a few minutes after Vanessa's shift. He apologized for being late and attributed it to a longer than usual workout session. Vanessa asked if the mechanic was able to work on the car with the money she had given him. His initial frown of what one would perceive as confusion quickly shifted into a smile and a nod. He said that she had given him just enough to have important matters taken care of. "Hey I haven't heard from Mya in over a week I want to run by there and check on her. She's not responding to any texts." Pierre adjusted his mirror as he thought quickly. He asked Vanessa if something had happened between them to give her reason to ignore her. Vanessa said no of course not. "The last time she didn't come to work for so long she had pneumonia a little over a year ago. I'm hoping its nothing like that. But this time she's not even texting me." Pierre replied to her that maybe it was best to give her space and let her surface at her own time. Vanessa disagreed. She was concerned and needed to ensure her friend was OK to ease her own mind. Pierre let out a sigh and agreed. Vanessa talked about her day and how the store had been so busy. She stopped speaking suddenly. "How did you know this was the way to Mya's house?" Without hesitation, Pierre replied that he'd often dropped off the friend that Mya had left the party with the night the two of them had met. He said until his friend purchased his own car, he needed a ride there and a few other places on a regular basis. "Dude should be helping us get this car fixed I gave him so many rides. Dude could have been paying me rent for that passenger seat." Satisfied with the answer Vanessa continued to ramble about her day. As Pierre parked, he recommended one last time that Vanessa allow Mya to reach out. Vanessa said it would only be a minute. She banged on the door several times. There was no answer. As Vanessa knocked, a neighbor passed. Vanessa asked the familiar face if she had seen Mya. The woman said she had not seen her in several days. This caused more concern for Vanessa. As she walked back to Pierre's car she began calling Mya again. "She could have just gone out of town on a random thing. You shouldn't let it rattle you too much Ness." Vanessa's frantic state began to rise. This was not like Mya at all. "I'm going to the leasing office to ask them if they know anything." Pierre failed at persuading her against it. The manager at the leasing office said he knew nothing of her absence. Vanessa asked if he would check her apartment. He agreed. As the manager and Vanessa walked back toward the apartment Pierre exited the car. "Ness I'm sure that man has other things to worry about. She might just be off the grid for a bit. Are you sure she wouldn't mind you in her house like this?" Vanessa turned to Pierre with a solemn face. "She is my friend and I don't know where she is." Pierre accepted his inability to deter her. The three entered the apartment. There was no sign of struggle. There were no major items missing. Pierre stood at the door as Vanessa and the manager went room to room. Nothing seemed out of order. There was food in the freezer. Mya's closet stood at normal capacity. Vanessa sat on the edge of her bed. She was afraid for her friend. The manager said that if she didn't hear anything she may want to involve the authorities. Pierre's head raised and his ears went back. Vanessa thanked the manager and walked back toward the front room. Pierre could see the anguish all over Vanessa. He grabbed her arms and rubbed them. He told her she was more than likely fine and that he'd reach out to his friend. "I haven't heard from him in a minute either. They could have just said screw it and flew somewhere on a random trip. Don't let it mess with your head. I'm sure she's just fine. Let's get out of here. We'll wait a couple more days and see if we hear something." Though Vanessa could not hide her concern she agreed to Pierre's sensible request. Vanessa again thanked the manager, and the three exited the apartment. Vanessa sat quietly as Pierre drove. Pierre insisted Vanessa convert her attention. "Hey, I didn't tell you. I got good news. I got locked in for a fight. Some undefeated fighter out of Chicago. I want you there." Vanessa shook her head in agreement. It was obvious to him that her attention was elsewhere.

* * *

Vanessa woke up early the next day. She checked her phone. Still no response from Mya. She looked over at Pierre. He slept soundly. She had not. "Hey what time are you going to train today?" She shook him out of his sleep. He responded he would go once in the morning and again at night. She told him she wanted to go back to Mya's apartment. He said there couldn't be any change from the day before. He suggested again to give it time. "Your friend that knows Mya have you asked him if he's heard anything?" He said he would ask him as soon as he woke up fully. Vanessa screamed at him. "Why are you so unconcerned about this? Why aren't you worried? Its been a week and no one has heard from her and you're acting like that's normal! Why aren't you helping me with this?" Pierre sat up in the bed. He said he would text his friend now and alert her if there was any new info. Vanessa thanked him but remained unimpressed by his level of concern. Later that morning Pierre dropped Vanessa off at work. He told her he'd be back before her shift ended. She told him she would work two shifts and not to come until later that night. She entered the back room of the store and tapped the shoulder of an employee. "I have a small emergency. I will pay you to cover half of my shift today. I'll be back before it ends tonight." Her co worker agreed. She downloaded a ride share app and selected a route to Mya's apartment. She went to the manager's office. Before she asked, he told her no new developments had come about. She told him she must have dropped her earring in her apartment. He sighed and escorted her to the apartment. His phone rang and he said it was important. She assured him, Mya was her best friend in the world, quickly showing him pictures of the two in her phone. His phone continued to ring. Vanessa took the key from him, and eased his mind, telling him she would find the earring and lock up as soon as she was done. He walked off to answer the call in peace. Vanessa stood in the front door of Mya's apartment. Her mission was to find some clue as to where her friend could have gone. The kitchen held no clues. Her fridge was still somewhat full. The milk had over a week until expiration. There was a wine glass on the counter. There was a half eaten dish of pasta in a to go container. Her trash was half full. Vanessa rummaged through the top of the trash. There was nothing out of the ordinary. Her living room was in ordinary condition. She flipped couch cushions. She looked through her entertainment center. She opened the drawers on the coffee table. The coffee table was so nice. Vanessa wondered when she had purchased it. It seemed to be rather expensive. Vanessa sat on the couch. She took a deep breath then looked around with fresh eyes. The items in her apartment were conspicuously nicer than the last time Vanessa had visited. The coffee table was beautiful. The rug on her living room floor complimented the ambiance of the room. The table alone had to have costed hundreds more than the one she had last. She tilted her head as she looked... really looked at the entertainment center. The TV was 84 inches. She had a high end sound bar as well. The entertainment center itself was a work of art. Vanessa went back to the kitchen. She opened every cabinet drawer. She found several bottles of wine. Mya had always had good taste. What she lacked was good money. She walked toward the bedroom. She realized in her frantic state yesterday she had not noticed how nice Mya's apartment was designed. She had two vases on two separate end tables. Vanessa pulled out her cell phone. She found one of the vases. It costed $300. Vanessa walked back into the living room and realized Mya had 3 of them. "There's not enough overtime in the world." Vanessa said under her breath as she frowned. She walked back in Mya's bedroom. As she sat on the bed looking around, she stood up. Her bed was bigger. She had purchased a new king size, pillow top bed. The frame was immaculate. She stood in the floor and spun around the room slowly with a deep frown. This was all wrong. She opened Mya's closet. She was floored by what she saw. There were dozens of pair of nice shoes. She picked up one of the boxes of red bottoms. Perplexed, she moved hangers in awe at the beautiful garments in front of her. She placed the shoes back which caused others to fall. Behind several boxes was a small safe. What in the world would Mya have to protect with a safe? Vanessa began to become nervous. The safe wasn't all the way closed. She opened it to find several envelopes. She opened one. The envelope had inside of it over $3,000. There were five of them. Next to the envelopes there was a black notebook. Vanessa took it from the safe and sat on the floor to read it. She opened it up on to random page. It read.

"This time it was easier. He just wanted to rub my body and talk about black girl tendencies. 'How come Black girls this. How come Black girls that?' Damn man you should have just dated a Black girl when you were younger! Some of these dudes are hilarious."

Confused Vanessa read more random inserts from what seemed to be a diary of sorts from Mya. *'He loved my nails! I cant believe he would pay me for that!'*- *'He really bought me these shoes just because I said I wanted them. I bet his wife's closet is insane.'* - *'Room service is over rated. In the movies it looks so great.'* Vanessa turned toward the front of the book. She read. *'I cant believe I did that. It wasn't hard. But it was a little weird. But its people doing that for a cheap date.'*- *'This man is so rich. He'll meet what ever price we set.'*

Vanessa turned forward several pages. *'I don't see why I have to give them a cut. I'm doing the work.'* – *'I cant believe that dude was so weird this time. I wonder why he is so stressed. I'd never be stressed if I was that rich.'* – *'They want more of the money. I wont complain too much I'm still getting so much of it. But still.'* – *'I cant believe he hit me like that. I know I messed up but how could he beat me like that.'* – *'I don't have anything else to bring them.'* – *'Ness wont believe me. I cant believe I let him meet her. She can't be a part of this.'* – *'This man was never nice. I was such a fool. None of them are nice. They never were.'* Vanessa turned several more pages. *'Ness take this money and get away from him. True Jubilee doesn't exist. I'm so sorry.'*

Vanessa sat on the floor reading the last few posts again. Mya was apologizing to her directly. Get away from him? They were never nice? What did Mya want her to find? She took the money and the notebook. She returned the key to the manager. The answers led to more questions. One statement stayed in the forefront of her mind. *True Jubilee doesn't exist.* Vanessa returned to work to finish her shift. Pierre was there to pick her up afterward. She asked him if he'd heard back from his friend about Mya. He responded that his friend knew nothing. Again he said he was sure she was just fine. She was sure now too. She was sure that Pierre and his friends knew far more than he divulged. Every conclusion led to a question in her mind. She offered the idea of going to the police. It had been multiple days. Pierre seemed flustered at the idea. He said it would be a waste of time. Black people don't get the same responses when missing person complaints are filed. Besides Mya was more than likely just blowing off steam and needed solace. He went on with his empty assurances. As he spoke, she heard nothing. He touched her hand. She felt nothing. As he spoke, she heard nothing. He touched her hand. She felt nothing.

12

Are you sure?

Tom excused himself from the room of staffers to take a call. "We need to speak soon. I don't know when I'll be able to get there. We'll be here in St. Louis for the next 3 days. No, he still seems to be functioning perfectly. We've not had any odd conversations no. They used open source code! Yes. Yes. I can arrange that. Very well. I can handle the scheduling. Call me when you land."

Henry entered the room as Tom walked back in. Henry sat near a staffer to ask about an upcoming event. Tom interjected. "Henry it may be best to stay here and let Stanfield bounce all over the nation for the next couple days. Us sitting tight for a bit will make it seem like he is out making moves of desperation. We'll go into the city tomorrow and greet some of the metropolitan workers. Visit the hospitals and one of the fire stations. Then we can go on to your old campus for an impromptu speech. Should go over great while Stanfield is in different cities pleading for a chance to bend ears. What do you say?" Henry saw no issue with Tom's change of plans. He always enjoyed visiting his old university in the heart of the city.

As the staffers planned the next two days Tom pulled Henry aside. "Fate is on our side my friend. You're not going to believe this. Canon is flying in to St. Louis tomorrow. If he can squeeze us in, I think it would be great to get a photo op with the two of you here in your hometown. Maybe he can even walk your old campus with you for a bit before he branches off. Could score great for us Hen." Henry agreed. What ideal timing. Tom turned to head back to the staffers. Henry's eyebrows raised as he called out to him. "Tom. Tomorrow he's flying in? Did he say what his main objective was? Why was he already coming here to St. Louis?' Tom, without turning fully to face Henry, turned his head back toward him and replied, "Who knows? Billionaires and their planes right?" Tom continued on to avoid further interrogation.

The day started as most of Candidate Semita's days did; structured. Henry and his team made appearances at two fire stations as well as 2 city police departments. The people were proud of their hometown hero. Henry shook hands with dozens of nurses, physicians and staff at two hospitals. When asked if he was concerned about Stanfield's push into the heartland with ads, he replied. "A commercial shouldn't be that influential on the American people. But if it is, you'll be seeing me on a Superbowl commercial this year if need be." The crowd laughed. Henry continued. "Governor Stanfield's commercials seem desperate. As opposed to speaking to his positives he chooses to create negatives against me. Where did I come from? That tired undertone continues to riddle through out his sad attempt to fear monger. Where I came from is where I stand at this moment. The mighty Missouri." The crowd cheered for Candidate Semita as he continued. "The commercials don't bother me. Next he'll say I'm an alien. The ads are getting more and more odd. They

85

are nearly 'demon sheep' level nonsensical. We're just going to continue speaking to the people about the issues of the people. Sensibility over nonsense folks. Sensibility over nonsense." The crowd praised Candidate Semita as he and his staff entered SUVs.

"You really can't fail when you're on your home field Hen. That soundbite is going national! Great win today. And we Still have the Canon endorsement today. Days like this create the kinds of gaps that can't be closed." Henry with his eyebrows raised, studied Tom's gleeful optimism. "We have still a year before the vote. Ample time to lose. Caution Friend. Caution."

* * *

The team parked and walked toward a large group awaiting their arrival. Most of the group were made up of current students and faculty. There were some reporters in the crowd as well that had been present as Henry greeted hospital staff moments ago. Tom walked a few paces behind the group as he sent several text messages. Henry's arrival to the center of the campus spurred several cheers. The students were elated and many of the staff were in awe. Before Henry could address the crowd, chants broke out. "Semita! Semita! Semita!" After several moments Henry raised his hand to calm the spirited bunch. "It's always so good to be home." Brief cheers erupted. "How is the best university in the nation doing this evening?" The crowd once again unleashed cheerful screams. Henry looked out amongst the people. He paused. He pointed at one young student and asked her. "Why are you here?" The student was stunned. The question was so unexpected. "I don't mean to embarrass you. But I want to know. Why are you *here*? The student replied to ensure she would attain a great education. Henry nodded his head and asked another student the same question. "You there with the Cardinals hat? Tell me. Why are you here?" The student replied he was there because he felt it was the best decision for his future. Henry nodded and spoke. "I respect both of those answers. A great education is pivotal in today's world. And the decisions you all make now will indeed mold your future. But I want more. I want to know why you wake up early. Study on Friday nights. Stress over Essays. Why do you all push yourselves to accomplish? Why do you not feel this time could be better spent enjoying your youth? Why did you choose this path? You. Tell me what drives you? Why are you here? What is it you're chasing?" He pointed to another student. The student replied. "I'm here because I want change the world and be rewarded for it, Sir." Henry smiled. "That's the most honest thing I have heard in some time. Many of you all are here for the same reason my team is fighting to get into office. You truly believe you can contribute positive change to the world. That's why you stay up studying, which you all had better be doing by the way...but that's why your free time goes to texts books and study groups. You feel you have more to contribute than what you've already seen. I agree. You all do. And even in this old age of mine, so do I. We all have so much more to contribute to our nation. Contribution. That is what we all share. That's what we do folks."

The crowd threw praises and cheers toward Semita who began shaking the hands of nearby students and faculty. As this occurred a faculty member asked the crowd for its attention. "We have another esteemed guest today on our beautiful campus. Ladies and gentlemen Adam Canon! Tom stepped aside as Henry turned to greet one of his oldest mentors. Cell phones flashed from students faculty and media alike. Security staff and several officers created space for the two. The energy was electric. The crowd loved the two together. Adam Canon shook Henry's hand and smiled. Henry Semita smiled back and pointed to the billionaire causing a second round of cheers from the crowd. Adam Canon placed one hand up toward the crowd to silence it. "How are the future leaders of our world doing this evening?" Cheers rang out. "I remember many years ago, receiving dozens of emails from a young motivated entrepreneur. I remember being impressed by his accomplishments at the time. I met soon to be President Semita when he was what...30? 30 or 31 years old. He and this guy here, Tom Ducomen. These two have been contributing to this fabulous nation for most of their lives through business, philanthropy, and now through government leadership. It is astounding to see Candidate Semita able to adapt and adjust to so much on the highest of levels. You all have no idea how impressive this is. None of us truly do! His mind is of a vastness unable to be curtailed. Be very proud that our great nation will be led by the Missouri man Henry Semita!"

Adam Canon smiled as dozens of cameras flashed. He raised Henry's arm and allowed him to reap in the praise. The two were then whisked away by tons of security. The two groups drove up 40 West toward Henry's Chesterfield home. Henry's team sat with Adam Canon for over two hours. Tom stood during the entirety of the talks. He asked Mr. Canon what he thought of Semita's ideas around STEM education for the nation. Adam paused for a moment. Henry raised his eyebrows while studying his idols facial expressions. Adam Canon was calculating his forthcoming statements. This didn't scream untruth. Adam's pause could express an appreciation for the weight of the matter. Henry concluded he could accept the incoming criticism. "It isn't bold enough. The U.S. needs an education overhaul. School choice from a enter left candidate will not only win you this election but it's just correct. U.S. female STEM degree attainment needs to compound over the next decade. We have STEM jobs throughout the nation unable to be filled. I argue at some point our under educated unable to fill these vital roles will cause a national security crisis. A multitude of these roles will be contracted and outsourced to foreign firms at a rate we should all be quite uncomfortable with. Engineers, mathematicians, virologists, and rheumatologists need to have parades thrown for them in the streets. We need to make these lifestyles appealing somehow. If your pragmatism is perceived as abrasiveness, then lead them abrasively into the future Henry." Many of the staffers jotted notes. Henry sat still eyebrows raised, staring at Mr. Canon. Tom watched the interaction between the two. He swayed his head from side to side as if he were reading an opponent's mannerisms in a poker match. Adam Continued.

"Much of my professional life is well documented. After I was kicked out of a company I helped found, I helped build Anima Corp. and several others. I brought to Anima, a mindset I had not had previously. Being booted from something I had previously built, only for history to show I was indeed right... well that taught me a valuable lesson. I learned being correct doesn't always matter. History tends to rewrite what and who is right or wrong anyway. In many ways 'right and wrong' are societal constructs. Attack then, any idea with zero doubt and zero hope. Keep with you the expectation it won't be received as you would want. Those your ideas are presented to may in the current moment in time, perceive them as wrong. Expect people's lack of understanding to cause dissension. Humans

89

fear what they do not understand. They always have. And often they do not understand the need for change. Do not hope for the masses to align. Yet expect still to win. Because you see what they do not. You see beyond the current constrictive labels of right and wrong. You see end results. I have learned to enter a thing with the highest of expectations yet with the lowest of hopes. Let them hope. You lead. Lead them to the results Mr. Semita. Allow time to determine right and wrong."

Tom, unable conceal an expression of utter shock, called a wrap for the staffers for the evening. Henry thanked any of them. Most of them stopped to shake hands again with Adam Canon before their departure. . In the driveway one of the staffers whispered to another. "Did you catch that? Canon's usage of them and they? The man spoke in third person omniscient. 'Humans fear change. Let them hope'? He is not one of us. He is God in his world." The other staffer, quietly responded. "Oh God no Melissa because I was too busy trying to wrap my head around letting time determine who and what is right and wrong. Only time? Only forward time? History shouldn't be used as a cautionary tale? We mere mortals have indeed been in the presence of a divine being or something. But I guess several billion dollars will do that to you." Melissa replied back. "No. No it won't. My family has dealt with billionaires. What we just sat in on. That isn't money. Money only gives a man so much. And money doesn't give you that. Power gives you that. Secrets give you that."

Tom, Henry and Adam Canon sat and discussed the campaign for a while longer before two of Adam's staff appeared from another room. "Mr. Canon. We have to be there in the morning by 9:30 sir. We should probably get going soon." Adam Canon nodded. He asked one of his men. "What's the status of Project Conundrum?" The staffer replied to Mr. Canon. "We expect to receive incoming information immediately Sir." The two men walked toward the door. Mr. Canon stood and shook hands with Tom. "You are doing stupendous work. Stay the course. This is life altering work. Remember this." Henry went to shake Mr. Canon's hands. Adam looked deeply into Henry's eyes. He held his handshake for a moment. "Mr. Semita. There isn't a day that passes I am not impressed by your abilities. You are my best decision to date." Henry offered a polite smile and thanked his mentor. As Henry began to pull away, Adam Canon firmed his grip and asked, "Just out of curiosity Henry. What did you eat this morning?" Tom's face froze. Henry casually laughed as he responded he'd had yogurt and almonds. Adam Canon let Henry's hand go and asked, "Did you enjoy the food? Are you sure?" Henry raised his eyebrows. He studied Adam Canon's odd increase of inquisitive energy. What was so exciting about yogurt? Henry replied. "The yogurt was enjoyable as yogurt gets I suppose. I'll send you a pack back to San Francisco my friend. I'm sure you'll love it too." Henry let off a defensive laugh. Adam Canon tilted his head to the side. "Love? Extraordinary Henry. Extraordinary. I'm sure I will love it indeed." Adam Canon left, leaving Henry and Tom alone. Henry turned to Tom. "Canon can be so odd. Brilliant people are truly strange." Tom laughed nervously as he watched Henry go to the kitchen. Tom was uncomfortable. Why must Canon pole and prod so brazenly? Why couldn't he have taken all the interactions of the day as case study enough that Henry was a perfect man? Before leaving, Tom told Henry they would be back at it tomorrow morning. Henry replied he had the schedule and would be ready for staffers by 8:30. Henry sat in his kitchen with a laptop mulling over campaign data. He looked at the yogurt he had selected. Adam Canon's question replayed in Henry's mind. "Did you enjoy the food? Are you sure?" Henry ate another spoonful, while thinking about the odd questioning. Suddenly he felt cold. He was freezing cold. He dropped the spoon on the floor. Picking it up he realized he was not actually cold. He was remembering *being* cold. He was overtaken with remnants of a memory. Henry clenched the spoon. His eyes were shut. He listened intently to the voice in his mind asking him. Who are you? Are you sure?

13

protégé

A thorough survey of one's future blueprint will always unearth remnants of one's past. The future is in direct correlation to one's past. Some build in order to replicate their past. Some build in spite of that past. Still the past is there. Julia painted. She painted in spite of her past. She knew memories would swell with every stroke of the brush. But she also knew she was safe. She was in St. Louis. She was far from California. She was with Christopher. She was far from that voice. So she painted her future, as she battled remnants of her past. The memories came more often now. As she would sketch, her mind forced her to remember. There was the television set again. Repeating hours of facial animations. The TV sound was off. She remembers sitting and being forced to simply watch. Watch and replicate. She remembered the countless hours of books being read to her in several languages. She could still recall every written detail of the Battle of Bloody Ridge in the Korean War. It and other historical facts had been inserted into her mind endlessly. Julia sketched as she remembered the cold room. It was so cold. There was no need for her to have to sit there and shiver. Those questions irritated her. She knew who she was. She was Julia Haywood. She knew where she was. She was in California. The packaging on one of the syringes next to her bed said so. She knew what she had eaten. Why did they continue to ask her these things? As she sketched, she grit her teeth. She could now accurately answer the one question she could not then. "Who am I?" She now knew. Julia remembered her answer at the time. She answered as she had been programmed to. "You are the creator. You are my savior. You are a friend." Julia stopped sketching. A tear fell from her eye. She was now aware none of these assertions were true. He was never a friend. The voice that controlled her circumstance in that small dormitory was never a friend. He had not saved her. He had stolen her. He had changed her. She was Julia Haywood because of him. Who she was before, he had altered. One thing was true though. He had created her. Julia stared at her sketch. She longed to remember herself before it all. She longed to remember any parts of her original state of being.

She couldn't be satisfied with the amount of information on her first experience. She longed to remember Robin Campbell. Often Julia wondered if Robin was a happy child before she died. Before Julia presumed much or her physical body. Moreover she felt fear. How would she be able to make Christopher understand who and what she was? Would he be afraid? Would he think she was insane? Worse still was her fear that he wouldn't feel for her again. Would he treat her like an experiment? She was technically just that. She sat and read the article on her cellphone again.

A fatal car crash claims the life of a family of three.

Julia read the article again. She was surely by now, capable of reciting the article by memory. She read for an untold time the

94

article of her family perishing in a car crash. The family was set to drive across the country. The family vehicle was struck by a truck. The parents, Mr. and Mrs. Campbell died instantly. The young teenage daughter was taken to a nearby hospital where she later perished due to injury.

On that fateful day in June Robin died and Julia was conceived. Julia sat staring at her original teenage picture in the article. Her eyes swelled with tears. She quietly wept for that girl and for herself. But the girl was her. Julia was Robin. Julia kept her blood, her eyes, her DNA. She just didn't have her memories. Her savior had stripped those from her. Christopher was a man of science and technological discovery. He would surely understand. He had to. She sat there staring at the article and wondered how her love would ever accept this deranged truth. Julia Haywood was as created as were the products Anima produced. In a lab. She was a human enhanced. Her mind used her organic neurons as any human. Her flesh felt temperatures as any human. All her senses were in tact. She loved the red wines and the dark chocolates Solo brought to her. But she was far more. They added to her central nervous system nearly 2 trillion transistors. Infused into her spine were microscopic nanometer chips that he and a trusted team had invented solely for her. For her and the two others like her. Julia's body had within it more technological advancement than the militaries of most advanced nations. She lacked the inability to process. She was incapable of being incapable. Julia was for all intents and purposes, one of the most powerful super computers that would ever be created. She possessed the powers of the vast human mind in addition to the very best of human ingenuity. Julia's life experiences were as all humans, downloaded into her mind and remembered. Julia though was incapable of forgetting anything.

Ever.

In all her enhanced engineering perfection, she was still very much human. She was still a woman. She understood how they created the three of them. Multiple essays textbooks and interviews of human psychology were input during their recreation. She could understand a man with a God complex. She fully comprehended duality and flawed logic. She could lecture on historic philosophers opposing viewpoints of the existence of free choice. But she was still a woman. She was a woman in love. Julia did not calculate falling in love with Christopher. She didn't even consider it. But she had. Her love for him caused the duality she very well comprehended. Her initial goal was destruction. She wanted the companies destroyed that allowed her to become. She wanted the virologists, the data scientists, biologists, neurosurgeons, pathologists and engineers all exposed. She wanted practicing licenses lost. Every entity that conspired in her new existence deserved to be bankrupted. Fitting as they were bankrupt morally. Above all Julia longed for the voice that haunted her to atone. She loathed how so many admired his accomplishments. He was no hero. She longed to have the name and legacy of Adam Canon destroyed. His scientific accomplishment poked fun at eternity. Robin should have been laid to rest with her family. But Adam Canon had concluded his own master plan qualified to usurp God. Julia wanted him humbled. Destruction was her goal. Then her plans landed her in Christopher's arms. Christopher was an honest and thoughtful leader of Anima Corp. He was unaware of his mentor's attempts to mock the cosmos. Christopher knew Adam Canon as most knew him. An innovative genius bent on changing the world for the better. Julia had reached duality. Julia realized Christopher's very being was intertwined with

Adam Canon's. To destroy the work of her enemy would be to destroy the soul of her lover. Julia had finally become a victim of quandary. She had not previously calculated man's most powerful variable. Love.

There were times she felt she could sit down with Christopher and tell him everything. Tell him that his mentor was mad. Tell him that Anima's technological advancements were used to reanimate lost lives against their will. Tell him that she should not exist. But Julia feared the possible outcomes so she refrained from these truths. Her fears would create a counter argument. Christopher loved her. And he loved Anima. He didn't need to be hurt by what he loved. He just needed to continue to love. He produced best when he loved. He had done nothing to not deserve blissful ignorance she would conclude. She sat in the apartment processing the opposing sides. Justice or Love. Destruction or protection. Revenge or adornment. She was a woman at war with herself.

Christopher was somewhat excited about EJ's boxing match. He wanted Julia to come with him to the fight. She declined repeatedly. She told him she didn't want to see two people punching each other for entertainment purposes. Christopher laughed as he expressed to her how surprised he was that the young fighter and his friend were both employed with Anima Co. This gave Julia pause. "The fighter and his best friend you are going to see, work here in St. Louis at Anima? They didn't know who you were until you told them Solo? How funny is that. How long have they been with Anima?" Christopher continued on about the pair and the gym and boxing as Julia processed the information. As Christopher chose a shirt Julia came into the room. "I don't want to stay in the house tonight. I think I will go with you. Let's see what this young Anima warrior can do." Christopher grabbed Julia and kissed her and began shadowboxing as she dressed. He was happy to have his two loves so intertwined. How deeply so, he had no idea.

Phil stood over EJ's shoulder. EJ listened to a motivation speaker in his headphones. His eyes were tightly closed. Phil's eyes were open and piercing. He watched everything around them as Eric went into the dark place fighters go before battle. Gordy supervised his assistant wrapping Eric's hands. Phil intently studied Gordy in these moments. Gordy muttered under his breath as Eric's hands were nearly wrapped. "Do it again. Start it over." The assistant instantly unwrapped EJ's hands on Gordy's command. Phil continued to watch Gordy. He longed to see the process as Gordy did. The assistant re wrapped EJ's hands. Gordy's lips continued moving inaudibly. Was he chanting? Was he praying? His eyes went back and forth between EJ's right and left fist. "Phil, break him out." Phil tapped Eric once on the right shoulder. Eric's eyes opened. Phil took the headphones of Eric's head. Gordy locked eyes with Eric. "He has come here to steal from you. In old times thieves were subject to the loss of an ear. Thieves were flogged. Thieves were publicly embarrassed. Some were even murdered. Because stealing dismantles a society. A man has no need to work if he can be robbed of all he works for. And if a man doesn't work society breaks down. This man has come to steal from you. Which means Eric he has come to destroy. Defend this house. Allow no destruction. He is a thief. Do with him what you will. Break him. Do you understand me Eric?" EJ stared intently at his trainer. "I do."

* * *

Phil and Gordy's assistant walked out in front of Eric. Gordy trailed directly behind EJ. His opponent, Hernandez was already in the ring. He and his team watched EJ intently as he entered the ring. Phil a seat closely behind Gordy's assistant. Phil was nervous for EJ. He knew EJ could win this or nearly any fight. He also knew EJ was prone to give in to his own temper. EJ looked across the ring at Hernandez. The ref bough the two together. The sound of the bell started the round. EJ threw two beautiful jabs both connecting with his opponent. The debate had begun. Hernandez shook off the two punches and returned fire. He connected with EJ with a left hook. EJ side stepped to avoid the jab he knew Hernandez would throw next. A fighter is most vulnerable in the brief moments after he's thrown a punch. Hernandez's missed jab offered a small window of time for EJ to throw a three punch combo. Hernandez was dazed. He took a deep breath and clinched with Eric. Gordy was ringside screaming at Eric to not let the fighter weigh him down. "Move that weight off of you Eric. Release yourself!" Eric threw a quick short uppercut to create space. When Hernandez took a step back Eric threw a fast cross to his eye. The crowd cheered. The round ended decisively in EJ's favor. Gordy told Eric he had won the round. Eric began to get excited in the corner. Gordy frowned at him. "I didn't say you won the fight. He is about to attack you now like a man possessed. He is going to show you hand speed now. Continue to articulate your main points. Do not be fooled into his change of subject Eric. You go in there you further elaborate your points you do not give in to a topic change. Keep the main thing the main thing." Eric stood in preparation for the second round. Hernandez came sprinting out of his corner with flurries of punches toward Eric. He threw every combination with desperation. Eric realized what Gordy meant after several failed attempts from Hernandez. EJ threw two combos to gauge his opponent's defense. Hernandez was too focused on making an argument to defend himself. Eric stepped back knowing his opponent would follow. With each whimsical step Hernandez irritation grew, and his energy lessened. Half way through the second round Eric noticed the hooks thrown were shorter. Hernandez had nearly punched himself out. Eric moved to his right. Almost on command Hernandez threw a cross. Eric bent his knees and hit him with a powerful uppercut. Before Hernandez knew he had been hit, Eric threw a hook with each arm. Hernandez fell to the canvas dazed and unable to continue. Phil and Gordy's assistant rushed into the ring to celebrate with Eric who stood motionless staring at Hernandez. The crowd cheered for him. Eric responded by lifting his right arm. As he and Phil walked back to the locker room, Phil pointed out a familiar face. It was Christopher Solomon. He pumped his fist and whistled as he nodded toward the pair. Eric smiled and pumped a fist back.

The announcer took to the ring. "Ladies and gentlemen. We have arrived at our main event." EJ turned back toward the ring. "Phil have you seen the fighter from Chicago that Pierre is up against?" Phil replied he had not. They both stood and watch as the Chicago fighter, Vaughn windy city Wendell entered the ring. There were faint cheers as a few supporters had made the drive from Chicago to St. Louis. Eric watched intently as Vaughn circled the ring. He looked calm and comfortable fighting away from home. The lights dimmed. Gordy's assistant walked past EJ and Phil. Behind him walked a stone faced Pierre. He stopped directly in front of EJ and spoke. "That fighter you just beat was a free lunch. Watch me bring in a real meal." Phil grabbed Eric's arm. Eric stood there confused at Pierre's aggression. Could Pierre's aggression be attributed to the fact he was moments away from battle? What would be the reason he would be abrasive with a fellow gym mate? Eric attributed it to a fighter's mindset before a clash. He watched Pierre and two of the gym assistants walk Pierre into the ring. Phil looked across the gym to notice Gordy. He wasn't directly in Pierre's corner. Phil wondered why. The two fighters came face to face as the ref went over the rules of the bout. Pierre smiled as he touched gloves with Wendell. As he returned to his ring Eric watched as Pierre's face altered. His smile vanished and his eyes seemed to light up. His face was blank. There was nothing there. The bell rang. Wendell walked toward Pierre who seemed to still be standing in his corner. Pierre pivoted left and Wendell stalked forward. Pierre threw the most pristine jab Eric had ever seen. Wendell was flush but continued forward. Pierre threw the same jab followed by a hook with the same hand. Wendell pressed forward to return the damage. Phil watched in awe at Pierre's complete control of all events in the arena. It seemed he could lower the temperature with a thought if he wanted. Pierre stopped pivoting and switched feet. This threw Wendell off his forward momentum, causing him to stop his forward motion. He offered two quick jabs toward Pierre in hopes of establishing his presence. It was of no consequence. The ring belonged to the Sultan. Pierre landed two more jabs on his opponent. This caused Wendell to respond by cutting into Pierre's space with two giant steps accompanied by a hook to Pierre's body. EJ watched as Pierre laughed the punch away. Wendell throw another hook to Pierre's body. Pierre pivoted into the punch. Eric quickly realized Pierre was allowing the contact. He was baffled. Pierre was baiting the fighter. Wendell threw a cross that missed Pierre's face and followed it with another hook to the body. The trap had been set. After this hook to the body, Pierre took a step back and threw a crushing hook to Wendell's face. Wendell's eyes shot open. Pierre again laughed at Wendell as he threw two jabs and back peddled away. As Eric watched the lessons Pierre taught, he admitted to himself, he had never seen such control of an event before. The round ended with Pierre in complete control. Gordy noticed Phil and Eric watching the fight. He wanted EJ to see Pierre in action. He wanted him to understand the science on a higher level, even if the lessons came from such a tainted vessel as Pierre.

The second round started. Wendell seemed angered with his performance in the first round. He set a pace in the second round in hopes Pierre would be unable to agree with. Wendell made a decision to sacrifice safety. He swung tight hooks to Pierre's ribs and backed up before the response. Pierre nodded his head as if to say good job. Pierre immediately landed two hooks to Wendell's body. Wendell responded with a job. He missed. Pierre weaved the jab with a calm routine head motion. Suddenly Pierre lowered his hands. The Lair's assistant trainer screamed at Pierre to keep his defense up. Pierre stood in front of Wendell and screamed at him. "Come on Chi Town have at it!" Pierre wound up both his arms and threw a left hook to Wendell's face. The crowd went wild. Everyone cheered at the showmanship displayed. Wendell's anger swelled as he threw flurries toward Pierre. Pierre danced through the punches. "You can't even hit me you lame." Pierre taunted Wendell for several more seconds of the round. "You're undefeated how?" Pierre laughed as he parried punches thrown. He back peddled and threw more perfect jabs. EJ realized Pierre wasn't even trying to hurt the opponent with the jabs. He was hitting him just to show him he could. "He's not trying to beat him Phil. He's already beat him. He wants to embarrass him." Phil responded with an inaudible *wow*. 15 seconds before the round ended Pierre raised his fists. He moved closer to Wendell cautiously. He began to throw beautiful poignant flurries. He landed at will. Wendell gasped for breath after taking a cross to the nose. Pierre turned and walked away before the bell sounded to end the round. As the crowd cheered, Pierre locked eyes with Eric. He mouthed the word *food*. Eric frowned. Rather he understood it or not, he was now aware. Pierre was no fan of him. Pierre wanted it known to all. The Lair was his. The College would never have a more prodigious student than he. The third round started. Most in attendance were now aware Vaughn Wendell stood no chance. Wendell's body language showed that he was too aware. He was outclassed. Pierre walked calmly toward Wendell and threw two punches, causing him to go into a defensive shell. Pierre immediately clinched with Wendell. Coming out of the clinch Pierre threw a powerful animal like left hook followed by a right uppercut. He ended with a right jab. Wendell fell several feet back before falling to the mat. He still had energy in his body, but his spirit was broken. Pierre screamed at him to stand up. Wendell sheepishly stood. The ref finished the standard eight count. He asked if Wendell wanted to continue. His mouth said yes. His spirit begged for the bout to be over. Pierre ran toward Wendell. He threw a faint with the left causing Wendell to bod toward the right. Right into Pierre's trap. Pierre threw a commanding right hook followed by a left cross and a left uppercut. Wendell dropped. The referee waived his hands. The bout was over. The Sultan reigned supreme once again. As the crowd cheered, Pierre turned toward the corner and stared at Eric. He mouthed again one word. *Food.* Gordy stood off watching the interaction between the two pugilists. The clash he didn't want he could now confirm would be inevitable.

Phil and Eric went over to greet Christopher Solomon and the woman he attended with. "Hey that was a hell of a fight Eric. You really controlled him mentally in there." Phil fist bumped Solo as EJ accepted praise. "Guys this is my gorgeous girlfriend Julia. Bug these are my STL Anima connections Phil and EJ." Julia smiled and shook their hands. "Hey why does he call you bug?" Christopher and Julia laughed as Julia explained she was a born in June. "She's my June bug." Phil and EJ smiled. Christopher and EJ talked further about boxing as Julia asked Phil about his time at Anima Co. He told her it was a cool job with great benefits. He expressed to her how funny it was to find that Solo was the CEO. Julia said that Solo traveled often for work and, though he wouldn't admit it, would need assistance at times. Julia felt Phil should take on a complimentary role with Christopher. Phil was surprised. He asked if Julia thought he would be an adequate fit. Julia replied. "Phil I think you are exactly what he is going to need in the future. How can I reach you if need be. You are after all his STL connection. Phil laughed and offered his cell info and an email. Julia paused. "You play video games at all?" Phil laughed as told her he and EJ of course gamed in their downtime. "Tell me everything about the system you use and write down your gamer tags." Phil replied he would text them at that moment. "No. Write them down Phil. Yours and Eric's. Write them on paper. Do not text them." Phil frowned and let off an awkward laugh. He wrote the gamer names on paper and gave them to Julia. She quickly put them in her purse. "Sounds strange I know. But I assure you It'll make more sense eventually. Thank you Phil." Julia smiled at Phil who shrugged off the awkward behavior and continued toward the back. Christopher and Eric continued chatting for a minute longer before Julia grabbed Christopher by the arm. The shook hands again as Eric walked toward the locker room. "Solo. I think Phil and Eric are underutilized. You should bring Phil on as your personal assistant. He seems so smart and humble. He can be your protégé like you were to Mr. Gregerov. Think on it?" Christopher wasn't opposed to the idea. Worst case scenario he would at least have a consistent workout partner.

14

mutual assured destruction

He sat alone in a booth reading a tablet drinking a coffee. Pierre sat watching him choose certain women in the room with his eyes. Pierre knew those eyes. He saw them often. His eyes exposed an all too familiar insatiable appetite. Pierre picked up his fruit and water and sat before him in the booth. He looked up from his tablet with a look of surprise and interest. Pierre spoke as he chewed his apple. "She wasn't as cold as the one by the door though" That's the one I wanted to get at. But I can never knock a man for having a type or three." Before he could muster an appropriate outrage, Pierre rose both hands to prevent a response. "I meant no disrespect. I just noticed the beautiful women. If men cant notice women anymore what the hell can we do? I just wanted to offer you my business card for a cleaning service me and some friends started." He looked at Pierre still visibly irritated but unable to hide a low level of interest. "Kid I have cleaners. I appreciate it. And yes the women were beautiful but if you don't mind I'd like to get back to my reading." As he looked down at his tablet Pierre lowered his head toward the table and leaned in. "Naw man I can assure you the services my cleaners provide are exemplary. I can guarantee you've never received such a high level of service from such a young pure staff like I can offer you. Have a look at some of the pricing models man." Pierre slid a cell phone toward him. The man glanced down and slid it back immediately. "Hey what the hell is wrong with you? Who are they and...do you know who I am?" Pierre placed one hand on the mans wrist and replied, "No sir. I have no clue who you are. I do not know who you are nor am I asking who you are. You seem to be stressed. Your mind seems cluttered. We offer the best de-clutter known to man. And that's what you are. Who you are is irrelevant to me. What you are is all that matters. You sir, well you are just like me and all the rest of the kings walking this Earth. You are hungry. Let your hair down and pick a meal." He sat back in the booth and frowned while looking Pierre in the face. Pierre sat back and bit his apple. There were a few moments of silence before Pierre re opened the image on the phone. "You're still hesitant because we just met. That's fair. I noticed your attention change as you saw different flavors so I'll pick for you." Pierre scrolled to a certain phone for a second, found the desired image and slid the phone back to him. "This is one of the best cleaning services you will find. Your de-clutter will be a thing of the past. And I can imagine your, your...what word am I looking for? Your what, your apprehension. Didn't you say earlier you'd be at the Grand Hotel in room...I forgot already I apologize. Here is the number to text with nothing but a room number tonight if you remember that room number. Try and remember it, say around 9:30 p.m. Again sir, I don't care who you are. I just care that you give my small startup a chance man. Be a man and live a little. Scratch that, go ahead and live a lot. Your concern is that clutter. After tonight You'll have zero concern." Pierre added a phone number into the notepad of his tablet, picked up his apple and walked away. He sat alone in the booth for 30 minutes, hand on his spoon while it was still in his now cold coffee. He stared at the number as the image of the young woman Pierre in the phone caused his mouth to salivate. Live a little. At 9:30 P.M. there was a knock on the door. The Jubilee co-founder opened the door and greeted a young beautiful woman. The night went well for both parties. She told him truths she didn't often tell the others. She told him of her plans and ideas. He offered advice to her and books to purchase. She told him she wasn't supposed to give her true number to anyone she would meet. He said it would be their secret. After their first night he demanded to see her weekly. She loved talking to him about his life experiences. Her body had purchased her a window into a world she would otherwise have little knowledge of. His shame dissipated after their fourth encounter. He deserved her beauty. He deserved her youthful energy. There was nothing left to be ashamed of. As she ate room service he grabbed her hips. "If you aren't comfortable saying it then by all means do not. But I'd like to know your real name. Your actual one, not the one you use with them." She was taken aback. She turned to look at him cautiously. He could sense the confusion and fear. "I will take the risk first. I'll tell you my real name. You'll tell me your real name. We'll both possess the power to destroy each other. This means we will both be forced to trust each other. Do we have a deal?" She laughed. She extended her hand to him. "We have a deal. My name, my real name is Mya. It is nice to meet you Sir." They shook on it and he offered his name. "We have now reached mutual assured destruction. One can not destroy the other's name without destroying their own." Mya laughed as she thought about the power he had bestowed upon her. She sat a moment in silence before asking him. "You did this why? You exposed yourself to me why?" He took a fork and hit it against a wine glass. He sat for a moment before replying to her. "The magnitudes of power are measured by the management of vulnerabilities. Also. Just because I could." Mya chuckled as she continued to eat. As she set to depart she turned to him. "Just remember Pierre can never know I gave you my real number or my name. He would be furious with me. Please never let this out. I don't know what he'd do to me." He hugged her and put an extra 500$ in crisp hundreds in her hand. He watched as she put them in the sole of her shoe before she left. He understood. The extra would always be a secret.

Over time Mya had amassed a great deal of cash from the co founder. He taught her how to set up accounts in other places far from St. Louis without having ever traveled there. Just in case. She did as she was told though she had no reason to think she would ever have reason to flee. He made it clear when she could text him. His wife of course. She understood. She enjoyed having one person she could be vulnerable with. One person that understood. One person that couldn't judge, lest he be judged. When he enjoyed her, she demanded to be herself. She demanded he call her Mya. She would ensure her name rang out in her ear. She felt powerful. He was powerful and in moments of lust she controlled him. She was powerful. In moments. And then there was a mistake. Pierre picked her up. He told her he had someone he needed her to see. She shook her head in understanding. He said he was a boring guy much like the Jubilee co-founder. He was set to be married and his friend had requested a proper send off for him. Without thinking Mya laughed and continued to speak about her days events. Pierre was sure she should have had questions. When he met with him again he asked. "Mya is still perfect for everything you need? I can introduce you to someone else if she's getting boring to you." Without thinking he replied, "No Mya's will do. Same time this Thursday." Pierre sat for a moment in silence. She had broken his rule. He combed over different scenarios as to how her true identity could have needed to be disclosed. He found none. He brought the issue to his business partner. Without hesitation he told Pierre this was unacceptable. If she would be comfortable breaking this rule she would be comfortable with so much more. If she could garner relationships with these men, then they wouldn't be needed. If she could build trust with them who's to say they wouldn't offer her exclusivity? Their sinister business model would be obsolete. Pierre realized he needed to make an example out of her. It was on this night that he beat her. He beat her in the hotel room with the door closed. He waited to beat her in the company of others. Another lesson in Power and vulnerability. He embarrassed her. He called her by her true name as he beat her. "Its Mya right? Yeah OK! Hurry up Mya!" As she cried she knew power was not for her. She would no longer lust after it. She knew for some reason he had betrayed her. And she knew after that night. Pierre reigned supreme.

* * *

Vanessa laid there next to Pierre. The words of Mya's journal replayed in her mind. *I cant believe I let him meet her. She can't be a part of this. True Jubilee doesn't exist.'* Vanessa still hadn't heard from Mya. She had hid the money. She had taken the journal. But the discoveries left her with more questions than when she began searching. Pierre woke up still speaking on his

110

victory over the once undefeated fighter from Chicago. Vanessa did her best to seem engaged. The disenchantment screamed at him. "Your friend will pop up eventually. I'm surprised you don't know where she is. You two seem so close. You cant think of anywhere she would have gone?" Vanessa silently shook her head. Pierre needed a change of subject. "Hey two more wins and I should have enough to get the car taken care of and pay you back! Almost there!" Vanessa smiled and replied that she was happy about the good news. She said she was going to shower. Pierre watched her energy as she went toward the bathroom. He knew that rather Mya turned up or not, he had lost her. But he still needed her. Or at least he still wanted her. She told him she would be home all day as he prepared for the gym. She asked again if he would reach out to his friend to check on Mya. He said he would. 30 minutes after Pierre left, Vanessa decided to go back to Mya's apartment in hopes of a clue. She assumed Mya was safe because of the amount of money she had. But she still needed to know where she was. And she still wanted to be sure she was safe. She caught the bus to Mya's apartment. She entered the leasing office. The same disengaged employee spoke from behind a computer monitor. "Listen, I still need to find my friend and I don't want to hear about your policies. I know you know I am not a thief and she is my genuine friend. So lets just get to the point. Let me in her apartment." The employee turned from the computer screen toward Vanessa. Before he could laugh her out of the office she showed 2 crisp hundreds. He handed her the key and begged her to be quick. She entered the apartment and went straight to the safe. It left behind no clues. She grabbed the journal. She realized there was so much left unread. She sat in the floor and started at the first page. Within about 19 minutes of reading she had found the insert she needed. *'He taught me how to do so much. This little house is so cheap and small but its mine. I can't believe I own a house! And not far from Mizzou. Wish I could have gone to school here. Not much but its still my piece of the rich land. This is so cool. I cant enjoy it though. Never can get away long enough. They'll never just let me go fully. Sucks. But at least I have somewhere to run to.'* Vanessa slammed the book closed. Mya was somewhere near Columbia Missouri. She remembered in high school when they both realized college was unaffordable and therefore unattainable. She remembered Mya rolling her eyes as fellow classmates spoke on which universities they would venture off to. It seemed like yesterday when Vanessa hugged classmates in the final moments of school. Some of them she had not seen since graduation. Elissa! Vanessa recalled she and Elissa exchanging information at the party! She was enrolled and living on campus there in Columbia. Vanessa anxiously called her hoping for a quick response. "Elissa. Yes hey its Vanessa. I have to ask you for a strange favor. I am so sorry about this but I have no better ideas. No I'm fine. Its Mya. Yes. I think she is somewhere near your campus and may be in some kind of strange trouble. Doesn't surprise you? What do you mean? Huh? Wait. You're in town? Yes pick me up here. I'll send my location. This is so huge thank you so much! No I wont be upset at all, you can tell me anything that you might know. OK I'll wait for you to come." Elissa agreed to come to Vanessa's location. She arrived rather quickly. Vanessa began to speak rapidly about how Mya had not responded to any communication in several days. Elissa rose her hand in attempts to calm her. "Ness. Before we go any further you need to know some things that it seems you don't know." Vanessa sat perplexed on the couch. "Your friend... well...there have been some crazy rumors going on about Mya for over a year now. She somehow got mixed up with some dudes. These guys are known for bad things Ness. I think I have to just say this. People have been saying Mya's been a highly priced escort for a while. And if she has truly disappeared that has to have something to do with it." Vanessa's blank stare confirmed Elissa's assumptions. She had been unaware. "Ness I'm sorry to have to tell you this. Someone threw a hotel party months ago back here in STL. They saw her being shoved through a parking lot with two guys and another older woman. She was crying and she looked like she had no choice at all. Someone else said they saw her with a much older White guy once and then again in the same hotel. These are rumors but..." Vanessa dropped her head. This explained her findings. The money. The expensive shoes Mya couldn't afford. "Elissa that still doesn't explain why she just upped and left like she did. I think she has a small house near your campus somewhere." Vanessa showed Elissa the entry. She read it over perplexed several times. All of a sudden she grabbed Vanessa's shoulder. "My piece of the Rich land! Ness I think she is somewhere on Richland Road east of campus!" Vanessa grew excited. Before she could ask, Elissa volunteered to drive them to look for her that afternoon. Vanessa agreed. As they left the apartment she turned to Elissa. "You said she'd gotten tied up with some dudes she shouldn't have. What do you know about them if anything?" Elissa replied she didn't know much. Just that one of them was friends with a local boxer. Vanessa shut her eyes in sorrow. She needed to hear no more.

15

The Path

"Listen Mr. Ducomen. You are not a fool sir. To have reservations about my on boarding is common sense. So please allow me to explain. I pursued there what I pursue here. The experience. I wanted then what I still want from all of this, not to make a king but to have an ultimate early career builder. So many doors would be open to me with the addition of presidential campaign staffer to my resume. If it sounds superficial and self-serving, that's because it is. My working for Stanfield had nothing to do with me believing in Stanfield. It had everything to do with me building myself. And before you judge this. Ask yourself how many of your current staffers are true believers. How many would fall on the sword for your candidate? Now how many are here because it was the best opportunity they could have hoped for? I think you know the majority fall into the second camp. I'm as much of an opportunist as whatever aide fetched your coffee for before this very face time Sir. Aren't we all?" Tom sat across from Ken Hess with a piercing look of mistrust. "Tell me why I need you. Stanfield didn't want you and he's behind in the poling. Why should we want you?" Ken sat still for a moment before responding. "Mr. Ducomen, I can not offer you secret intel on the Stanfield campaign. I can't show you his next attack ad. I do not possess his tax plan although we can all guess who it would help. I can only say this. I have seen how they operate and its sloppy. He doesn't listen to his greatest minds. He lacks the ability to compromise. Either that or he just refuses. Why do you need me? Because I can tell you exactly how and what he thinks on every turn. Because I was one of them that had to think for him Sir. That's what I have." Tom thumped his coffee cup with his index finger. He looked up to a familiar face and caller her over. "Megan he will report directly to you. The very moment he bears no fruit, you will chop the tree. Get me?" Megan gave Ken a look over and nodded her head in agreeance with Tom's command. The two shook hands as Megan took Ken away. Tom watched from afar as the staffers chatted ate strategized and typed. He thought about Ken's words. He surveyed the group wondering which of them were opportunists and which were true believers. He wondered. Could any of them be both? His thought was interrupted by a staffer and Henry Semita walking into the office. Henry stood in the middle of the floor and requested the group's attention. "Everyone give me just a few moments. I want to say how proud I am of you all first. I appreciate the sacrifices you all have made for this most important work. I don't want you all to get overly anxious with what I'm about to say. I'm going to take the next 72 hours and do some much needed introspection and reflection. There is again, no need for concern. I promise not to return barefoot with a flower in my hair. But I am in need of time alone before we enter the home stretch." The crowd chattered amongst themselves. Tom stood up from his seat. He was more than surprised. He was afraid. Henry continued. "Some of you need to get a break as well. There is nothing like a refreshed mind to better commit to an upcoming task. Go home. See your folks. Go to a movie. Do you kids still go to the movies? Well stream one. Hit a beach. Do something for yourselves. We will be back to work here Thursday. Thanks team. That's all." The staffers looked around at one another before gathering their items and heading towards the exits. Tom waited until the room was mostly clear. "Hen what's going on? Are you feeling alright? What do you mean introspection? What made you do this? We can get a private physician if you're feeling ill. We can keep that out of headlines. Talk to me old friend what is going on?" Henry waited for Tom to calm himself. He responded simply, "I'm fine. I am just taking some time. I'll be in contact soon." Henry left Tom standing in the middle of the office. Henry grabbed a staffer on his way out. "I have what you asked for Mr. Semita." The staffer handed Henry a piece of paper. Henry thanked him, placed the paper in his pocket and left. When he was back home, he reached in his pocket and pulled it out again. It was just what he had requested.

Tom sat in the office alone. All of the campaign staffers were gone. Henry was gone. He'd be gone for three days. It was clear he wanted solace. He wasn't used to Henry breaking protocol without clear reason. Tom realized Henry had intentionally decided to not disclose his plans. Henry had decided. Of course he was capable to decide but Tom was unsure of what to do about the fact that he'd finally exercised the option to. This unnerved Tom. Henry had decided. The very sentence caused Tom a massive migraine. The quiet of the office caused his concerns to attack him. What if this were to happen once Henry had taken office? What if something was wrong? Tom had seen Henry operate so pristine for so long. Tom began to panic. He couldn't believe that after so many years Henry had surprised him. He realized he would have to make the call. " We need to speak. I'll come to you."

Tom sat in a dimly lit room. He was tired from the flight. Mentally weary really. But he had no time to succumb to jet lag. He came straight away to discuss the pressing matter at hand. Henry. A butler opened the door to the room Tom sat in. "Mr. Ducomen, Mr. Canon would like for you to follow me please." Tom followed the servant through the mansion and to an elevator. Tom watched as the servant pressed for the basement level. As the elevator arrived the servant got off. He turned to Tom and told him, "No sir. You stay on. Good day sir." Tom stepped back into the elevator which showed to already be on the last level. The doors closed. The elevator's panel turned a brilliant green. The elevator began to go down beyond the floor shown. Tom looked up at the camera above him and rolled his eyes. The elevator door again opened. Tom walked out to Adam Canon standing before him. "Come along." Tom followed Canon down a long corridor and through a door. The floor was constructed masterfully. Tom walked through the part of the sprawling space that mirrored a top tier hospital wing. He looked to the left trough a glass at a neatly prepared operating room. Adam Canon turned down another hall and led Tom through a lab. They entered a room Mr. Canon had designed as an office. The office had several monitors that showed different areas of the floor. One monitor showed the operating room just down the hall. Another showed a comfortably designed room with a large television and multiple books. Two more monitors showed the lab area just beyond the door. One monitor was turned off. Tom took a seat on a couch in the office. Adam Canon sat across from him. Tom pulled out his phone to turn it off.

"No need Tom. There is no outside signal here. Your GPS wont even show here. You're fine. I assure you." Tom put his phone back in his jacket pocket. "He has never ever done this. He's never done anything close to this. What the hell does time for introspection even mean Adam? Is there any chance at all that the original memories could be reestablished? And how does he have all that technology in him and never seem to malfunction? A fool I am obviously for now after so many years having so many concerns but still." Adam sat back in his seat. "Tom. The original memories should never be able to resurface. The mind in Henry is a new mind. The advancements in him I assure you would cause parabolic growth in the NASDAQ markets even if they were unveiled over a decade. Of a few things I am certain. One of them is, mechanically he is incapable of *malfunction.* But Tom remember Henry is still very much so human. Even with the transistors that offer him infinite learning ability and remove the capability to forget fact, he still posses every human emotion you all possess." Tom took a deep breath and shook his head while looking at the floor. "So, basically I am supposed to accept that the most advance creation in human history just got moody out of the clear blue. Mr. Canon, you know as well as I do the stakes at this level are unprecedented. I have been superb since you chose me in undergrad for this most unusual journey. And that's because I have been able to guide him through trust and results. Whatever he and I have set out to do has succeeded. Now we are in the hunt for the highest official office in the world and he changes? Maybe this is too much?" Adam stood up and walked to a small fridge. He took out two bottles of water. He tossed one to Tom and sat and opened the other for himself. "There is no amount of pressure for him. If the task has an answer he is capable of dealing with that task. He will be president. He is not malfunctioning. He simply may be in an emotion state. He is after all single Tom. Maybe he is bored. You get bored. I imagine you frolic with interns when you're bored. Or maybe you play cards or checkers. Inside that body is technological advancement and pure scientific wonderance. And also flesh and blood. He just may be in a mood Tom. As we all have been. He is not a laptop that would need a reboot. He is our next president of the United States. I am more than confident he can handle the pressure of him pursuing the highest official office in the land. Do you know why? Because I and multiple other of Earth's most impeccable minds created him to handle said pressures. Here. In the highest unofficial office in the land. Tom, I respect your concern. I appreciate it. Had you no concern It would be quite telling that you don't comprehend the stakes we are operating at. But Henry is perfection literally personified. Let him be human...at times." Tom took another deep breath. He had trusted Adam Canon's judgment since he was approached in undergrad. He was presented with what would be briefly described to him as the most unusual and incredible opportunity he would ever receive in all his years. With no further detail he eagerly accepted. He sat on the couch listening to Adam Canon go on about Henry's inability to malfunction. As Adam spoke, Tom recalled his introduction to the series of life altering events. Adam Canon had hand selected Tom Ducomen at the start of his first year in graduate school. Tom signed several Non Disclosure agreements before he was even allowed to meet Canon face to face. All of the formalities intrigued him more. He knew before their first conversation he would accept whatever the opportunity was. Adam Canon spoke quite frankly with Tom upon their first meeting. "I and a specialized team have regenerated a human corpse. Three to be exact. One will be

119

entering Grad School with you. He is oblivious to what he is. All he knows is the personal history I have constructed for him. It is as real to him as yours is to you. His assigned parents will tragically die within the next nine years. He has wealth and education. He is the most powerful invention walking this planet. And you are going to befriend him. You will attempt to conquer the world with him. Your personal gain will surpass many of your classmates as you are already quite well educated, but I will also ensure you have an additional 5 million dollars for every seven years you are in close relation to him. He is smarter than you and most anyone else. He is also unaware. He thinks he is as flawed as you and I. But he is impervious to flaw. And you will be his right hand. While unaware of the true nature of his own existence, he will lead humanity to a better one. He is the path. So I have named him Semita. His name is Henry Semita." Tom remembers his eyes growing wide. He remembers how he began to laugh in the face of the brilliant Canon, before reading his face. He was sincere. "Seven million. Half in various shares of companies you chair and influence. Every seven years." Tom's counteroffer was accepted within seconds. Tom Ducomen in that moment had become one of the most powerful men of his time. And could never tell a soul. As most with true power cannot. Adam Canon smiled as Tom departed that night back to Yale. He was quite confident that Tom was satisfied with his new role. But not more than Adam himself. Adam's most difficult feat had been accomplished that night. He had appointed a Jonathan to his David. Tom's mind snapped out of the reminiscent moment when Adam called his name. "Tom. Tell me now more about the HER you all viewed at that high school in Pennsylvania. Open-source code you say?"

* * *

Drew Xi put several books in his locker. He was excited about the study free weekend. His brother would be in town from MIT and the two would be spending quality time at home. Quality time for the pair would be them in separate rooms playing video games on separate systems while on the same team. Drew couldn't wait to be home. A classmate asked him what time he'd be logging in for a nightly video gaming session. "Dude I am on my way straight home. As soon as I carb up I'll be texting you to log on dude." Drew slammed his locker and headed for the exit to his bike. His phone rang. The screen said restricted so Drew rejected the call. As he jogged toward the bike rack it rang again. He frowned and decided to answer it. "Mr. Xi. Its Henry Semita. We met months ago. Look to your left." Drew, shocked, looked to the left toward the main street to see a Black SUV in the line of vehicles parked to pick students up. A window rolled down and a cell phone was shown. "We need to speak again. Today Mr. Xi." Drew left his bike and walked toward the SUV. As he walked up to the driver's side rear door, the window rolled down. "Hi Drew. Hop in. I'd like to speak further about a few things."